Testimony

By Peter Lazare and Sarah Lazare

WASHINGTON D.C.

Managing Editor: Troy N. Miller
Cover Designer: Jim Cooke
Copy Editor: Alex Abbott
Production Editor: Paige Kelly

Published in the United States by Strong Arm Press, 2021

www.strongarmpress.com

ISBN-13: 978-1-947492-54-7

For Mom

Disclaimer

This book is a work of fiction. While details from the broader political context are real—for example, the build-up to the Iraq War, and the existence of the Illinois Commerce Commission—all characters, events, and incidents in this book are either the product of the authors' imaginations or used in a fictitious manner. Any resemblance to actual persons, living or dead, or actual events is purely coincidental.

Before Peter Lazare passed away in November 2018, he wrote a draft of a novel.

Sarah Lazare, his daughter, spent two years following his death adding to and editing the manuscript, viewing it as a writing collaboration.

While this book is a product of both of their labor and visions, Peter did the hardest part: writing the first draft.

Table of Contents

Chapter 1

Sam was sweating in the best cheap suit he could afford. Walking down State Street in Chicago, his plan was to enter every restaurant, retail store, coffee shop, and tourist trap in the Loop. Three months out of work and all the goodwill of family and friends pissed through, he was down to skipping meals. He had just left what he thought was a decent impromptu interview with a burly man named Desmond at the Green Door Tavern. Cook, waiter, bar back, it didn't matter.

Almost a year removed from the global justice movement he'd walked away from right after 9/11, the last thing he wanted to be reminded of was that yet another war was on its way. Walking just past State and Monroe, he heard a familiar voice call out to him.

"Sam fucking Golden." He turned—it was Francis. A nice kid, too hippyish for Sam's taste, but a true believer. He stuck through the hard times, Sam thought. "What's it been, six months?" said Sam.

"Almost a year," Francis replied. Sam kept walking, Francis following behind.

"What's with the suit, man? You some kind of life insurance salesman?" said Francis.

"Trying to find work, waiting tables, bar back. Ever since I left, it's been…"

"Yeah."

"Listen, I'm trying to get at least twenty-five applications in this afternoon. Let's grab coffee sometime later this month."

"Of course." Francis gripped Sam's shoulder, and both stopped walking. "Man, it is so good to see you."

"Thanks," said Sam.

"So goddamn good to see you."

"I got that. Thanks."

"Why don't you join us? It's not a protest, protest yet, but some of us are canvassing the street corners to prep for a big march in February. Getting the word out. That cocksucker Bush is—"

"Francis, man."

"Yes, Sam-I-Am?"

"It's going to happen no matter what you do. Didn't you learn that in five years of doing this shit, no matter what we do, we're just pissing in the wind?"

"What happened to you?" said Francis. "We need people like you out in the streets now more than ever."

Sam patted the backpack he'd bought at Goodwill, now filled

with resumes. "I turned thirty, is what happened. Listen, good luck to you, really. I still support you, I'm just—out. You know this."

"Okay, well, will you at least take this? We're mobilizing for a big action in February." Sam looked at the flyer. "No War!" was written in heavy black font at the top. Below that, an image of the globe, a black flag emerging from it that said in white text: "The world says no."

"Yeah, sure, I'll hold onto this." Sam shoved the piece of paper into his backpack and gave a smileless nod before ducking into a Starbucks.

***

A week later, Sam lay on his couch, his clothes soaked in sweat, bare skin sticking to the cheap leather exterior. Over the blaring fan, he could hear the jingle of an ice cream truck, and the high-pitched voices of children shouting for it to stop. This was summer for them, but for Sam it should have been a work day. Instead, it was day ninety-seven of looking for a job—and, after pressing send on his fifteenth application of the day, he was taking a break.

The sound of his phone startled him, and Sam looked down to see a number he didn't recognize. Was this another collections agency calling about a medical bill he didn't know he had? It always amazed Sam how hospitals, legally required not to turn anyone away, are the quickest to run to collections when you can't pay. He let the call go to voicemail.

"Hi, I'm trying to reach Sam Golden," he heard a woman's voice on his answering machine. "My name is Dee Dee Schaefer, and I'm with the Illinois Commerce Commission. I'm sorry it took us so long to get back to you, but we'd like to interview you if you're still interested."

"Holy shit!" Sam shouted, jumping to his feet. Of course he remembered this job opening—a depressing gig under normal circumstances, but on this Monday afternoon, a god-damned beacon. He gave himself thirty seconds to catch his breath before turning off the fan and calling her back. "Yes, I should be able to make an interview in Springfield tomorrow, just let me check my calendar," he said, checking his nonexistent calendar—he didn't know why he was miming one. "Yup, okay, that should work."

Sam hung up the phone and bolted down the narrow stairway, squinting as he opened the door and ran onto the sidewalk. He shuffled in his pocket for some change, but just as he found it, the ice cream truck turned the corner. Ah well, he thought, it's too soon to celebrate. But as he walked back into his apartment, he couldn't stop smiling.

***

The next morning, Sam woke up an hour before his alarm went off, ironed his only suit, and spent a full twenty minutes shaving. The face in the mirror had small blue eyes crowned by bushy black brows the same shape and color as his hair, which frizzed up like a clown wig in the heat. He had a firm jaw and olive skin, with cheeks that were hollower than they had been six months ago, and stood at a willowy six foot one.

He got into his car for the 200-mile drive from Chicago to Springfield, praying to no one in particular that, if his car had to break down, it happened on the way back. He drove past corn and soybean fields, a smattering of gas stations, and fast-food restaurants. Sam couldn't help but compare the flat monotony with the hills and forests of Stamford, Connecticut, where he grew up playing in the ravine behind the Jewish Community Center. How did I wind up in this shithole state? came the familiar question. But this time, he noted this shithole might have a job for him.

When he pulled off of the highway, he was greeted by a large billboard showing an eagle perched in front of a faded American flag background. "Never forget, brought to you by Arlington Roofers," it read. Behind, a row of billboards—Subway, Sunrise Café, Oasis Nail Salon, New Life Church—vied for space with giant American flags hoisted on polls, each taller than the next.

Sam entered a residential neighborhood. At first glance, the houses appeared wholesome—with American flags, porches, and lawns, some ringed by trees. But when he looked closer, Sam noticed one had boarded-up windows, another had a porch with a collapsed floor. One light-blue house had shingles missing from its black roof and bushes that were so overgrown they nearly blocked the front door. Unlike the working-class Mexican neighborhood in Chicago where Sam lived, here there were no children playing outside. There was no one outside at all, just cars driving by.

In about three minutes, he was already downtown, such as it was. Sam found a parking space and gave himself one last look in the rearview before heading in. The Commission was housed in a century-old, ten-story building that looked like it had once been a hotel. The conversion seemed sloppy and cheap, with plain windows surrounded by plywood that clashed with the original brick exterior. Once in the lobby, Sam stood on a dirty carpet under a dropped ceiling surrounded by plastic wall panels.

He told the guard behind a desk the purpose of his visit. The guard squinted at a spreadsheet then pointed to the elevator ahead. "Fourth floor."

Emerging from the elevator, Sam saw a sign that said "Rates Department" above an office door. Sitting behind a large, curved desk, adorned with a small teddy bear and a framed photo of two children, a forty-something woman with bleach-blond hair was talking on her cell phone. She was plump, with a pleasant face and aviator glasses, the kind that were popular when Sam was a child. The secretary glanced up at Sam and gave him a smile. "Got to run," she said into her phone. "See you later, Mom."

"You the 2:15?"

"I'm sorry, the wh-what?" Sam stammered.

The secretary wrinkled up her nose. "What time is your appointment, hon?"

"Oh yeah, sorry, 2:15."

"I'm Dee Dee," she said. "You have your resume?"

"Yeah."

"Put it on the pile." She pointed to a mound on her desk. Sam pulled the piece of paper out of his backpack and before he set it down, he looked at the resume on top. Harvard graduate, summa cum laude. University of Illinois at Urbana-Champaign, PhD in economics. I may as well just pack my bags and go home, he thought.

"Why don't you have a seat?" said Dee Dee. She spun around in her chair and shouted towards the open door on her right. "Hey Charlie, your 2:15 is here."

Sam looked behind him and saw a tattered brown couch, a man sitting on the middle cushion, a woman sitting on the far one. They looked like they'd bought their clothes from down-

6

town Chicago department stores, and not even the clearance rack. Sam looked down at his own suit and straightened his tie, made of a thin polyester material he hoped would pass as silk. Not having to worry about how you are going to pay for rent, or your next grocery bill must be a peculiar feeling of freedom, Sam thought to himself. He knew from his political education that this was true in a Marxist sense—you can't really be free if you're unhoused and hungry—but now he internalized it on a gut level. And sadly, he thought to himself, he could not credibly blame bombing another job interview on capitalism. It didn't take a Randian acolyte to see, as his poverty dragged on into his early thirties, that his piling credit card debt was maybe less a product of class oppression and more him just being a fuck up.

He sat down on the empty cushion and pulled out a water bottle from his bag. There was just a sip left, and he downed it in an instant. He leaned back and tapped his foot while slowly peeling the paper wrapper from the bottle, not bothering to look where the pieces were landing. The loud crackling noise filled the room as Sam's gaze wandered to the floor.

He saw feet in worn, Velcro-fastened sneakers. When he looked up, a man was standing over him. He had black hair that faded into silver at his temples and a smile that sent wrinkles rippling across his face. He was wearing a jumper the color of a Girl Scout uniform and pushing a large garbage can on wheels.

"Oh, sorry," said Sam, as he reached down to pick up the pieces of paper that had fallen like confetti around his feet.

"You applying for the job?" the man said. Sam pegged his accent as Filipino.

"Yeah, rate analyst. Guess you can tell I'm a bit nervous."

"You can tell a lot about people from the trash they leave behind, yes." The man knelt down. "Don't worry. I'll get it."

7

Sam reached out his hand. "Name's Sam."

"Angelo." He gave a light shake then picked up the paper shreds.

Sam heard a man who sounded like he'd been woken from a nap grumble, "Okay, send him in." Dee Dee gave Sam a brisk nod, and he walked into the office.

Sam found a thin, bald man in his early fifties wearing a white shirt and red tie parked behind a desk stacked high with magazines and newspapers. The man looked up. "Charlie Harper, director of the financial analysis division," he said, extending a pale hand. A name as plain as the drive here, Sam thought to himself as he shook back, marshaling a smile of excitement.

Charlie motioned for Sam to sit then began reading from a sheet, starting at the top and working his way down. At first the questions were easy: "Why do you want this job? Tell me about your experience." But they became more difficult as Charlie proceeded. "Are you familiar with price elasticity? Marginal cost?" I mostly know this, thought Sam, as he rustled up responses.

"Now it's time for your test," said Charlie, bringing Sam into a small adjacent room, where he motioned towards a computer. Jesus, what test? I should have prepared better, thought Sam. My mother's right—I'm too sloppy, always cutting corners, not fastidious like my brother. "Here are some revenues and billing units for various classes. Figure out what the rates would be for each class."

Sam began to sweat as he opened Excel. Sure, he may have fudged his resume a bit, but that had always worked out for him in the past. The last time he had a job like this, seven years ago, he had to sprint for the first month to catch up to the person he claimed he was on his application. And his bosses didn't fire him, although they did load him down with grunt work—data entry, package deliveries, fetching coffee. But that was a left-leaning economic consulting firm in Chicago, willing—even happy—to hire an "avowed Marxist," as his boss liked to put it, a sarcastic emphasis on the word "avowed," as though the category itself was a joke, something that one grows out of but makes an interesting anecdote at a dinner party.

At least they were happy—until he quit to join the WTO protests in Seattle. He'd always been a socialist, but he'd dropped everything to join a global justice movement shaped by anarchist organizing structures—the affinity group, the spokes council— because it was filled with a hope and foolhardy ambition he'd never tasted before. There was this sense that you were part of something big, that militant union rice growers in South Korea and Zapatistas in Chiapas were on your side even though you hadn't met them yet. It was hard for him to explain to people who hadn't been there, but you could feel the presence of millions in those stuffy rooms where hundreds sat on the floor, the scent of B.O. filling the air. It was the closest to international class struggle he'd ever gotten, and it was enough to convince you that you and your rag-tag crew—armed with bandanas soaked in vinegar and a legal number scrawled on your arm in Sharpie—could take on the most powerful forces on earth, and win. And he'd adapted to, and even come to love, the frustrating horizontalism of three-hour-long meetings of hundreds packed into a convergence space, the hand signals it had taken him weeks to learn but which he now knew by heart, even though he wasn't sure when he'd be using them again.

Sam pinched the ridge between his eyes. Concentrate, he told himself. No matter what, you have to finish—to turn in something. Thirty minutes later, Sam attached the document and pressed send, then walked back into Charlie's office.

"Any questions for me?" Charlie asked.

After a long pause, Sam blurted, "How long is the typical workweek?"

Charlie's face became serious. "To be honest, we are swamped around here. Absolutely swamped. I personally have been putting in fifty to sixty hour workweeks for the last six months. I would expect the successful candidate for this job to do the same. Anything else?"

Sam exhaled "no," then stood up from his chair.

"Just one more thing before you go," said Charlie, and Sam sat back down. "We're part of a public-private partnership with United Gas and the FBI to report any suspicious, al Qaeda-like activities targeting critical infrastructure. How would you feel about monitoring this office? How can I trust that, if you saw something, you'd come to me?"

Sam rubbed his hands together. He thought about the long drive back, the odds of his car breaking down, the hot apartment that awaited him. The possibility, however slight, that this job could be a ticket to chipping away at his crushing medical debt, even if that meant a mundane twenty years working towards a pension and a fishing hole in Minnesota.

"Twelve thousand dollars divided by sixty months over five years," he found himself doing the math in his head instead of answering the question he'd been asked. He could pay off his medical debt and actually live like a normal person, or at least what he thought normal people lived like. No more revolution just around the corner only to find another corner and another like a dorm room Esher poster. Changing the world was exciting, to be sure, but the thought of stability, lake houses, and potato salad didn't sound so bad.

He swallowed and then said, pronouncing each word, "I'd be happy to keep an eye out. These are dangerous times, and you can never be too careful."

"Thanks so much, I've got a meeting to run to," said Charlie, jumping up. "Have a nice trip back." He dashed out and left Sam sitting alone in the office.

On the way out, Sam saw that Dee Dee was again on her cell phone. She flashed him a brief smile and he trudged off to the elevator to begin the long trek back.

The ride home seemed longer, and Sam couldn't stop replaying that last question—and his response. No, of course he wouldn't monitor that office, he assured himself. Never mind the ridiculousness of looking out for al Qaeda in every dark alley of rural America, Sam had long ago learned to distrust law enforcement. He'd been on the receiving end of too many police dispersal orders, followed moments later by the crash of batons and the spit of tasers.

He'd never forget when the rowdiest and most daring member of his anti-WTO affinity group was exposed as an FBI informant after he testified in a case out West—brazenly showing his face to the news cameras, a middle finger to his old comrades. Sam would never be like him.

Sam made it home as the sun was setting and found a space right in front of his building. He bumped the cars ahead and behind him as he settled in. "Take that, asshole," he muttered, not sure who exactly he was directing his anger at.

On the way into his apartment, Sam reached into the mailbox. An overdue heat bill, another letter from the hospital. Sam had been planning to call his mother to let her know he'd finally had an in-person interview. He'd already imagined her high-pitched, "Knock'em dead, Sammy." But instead, Sam took off his suit and tossed it on the floor by the couch. He lay down, turned on the fan, and went to sleep.

***

Three months later, Sam was waiting tables at the downtown TGI Friday's when he got a call from an unrecognized number. During his lunch break he sat down and counted his tip money, just forty-five dollars four hours into his shift. In the background, he could make out Chris Matthews on the breakroom TV, dumping on his old friends.

"These IMF protesters out in the streets, do they hate America?" Matthews smirked.

"Well yeah," Sam thought. "But not for sport."

Someone preposterously named Cliff May responded, "Yes, I'm afraid a lot of them do. They hate America. They align themselves with Saddam Hussein. They align themselves with terrorists all over the world. Anti-Americanism is in the air."

Before he could turn and yell at the screen, he suddenly remembered the strange call. Right—he was blocking all that out of his brain. Before checking his messages, he dialed.

"Illinois Commerce Commission, Dee Dee speaking."

What the hell? Sam thought. Why was she calling him months after he'd bombed that interview? "Uh, Sam Golden here."

"Sam! How are you? Let me put you through to Charlie."

Charlie didn't waste any time. "You still looking for a job?"

Sam touched his thumb to the tip of his forefinger on his

right hand, a habit he formed a few months ago after a burn left his nail deformed (he'd learned his lesson from the last time and hadn't sought medical care). That was during his brief stint as a line cook. He was quickly able to move to front-of-house, but all of his Mexican and Salvadoran coworkers stayed in the back. "When I didn't hear from you I thought you hired someone else."

"We didn't secure the finances to fill the position until a month ago, but we're finally in the clear."

"That's, um, wonderful news," said Sam, realizing his voice was an octave higher than usual.

"I want to be very clear about what your job will be. A rate analyst examines rates and costs of service for electric, gas, and water utilities. The analyst attempts to create cost-based, fair rates that protect the ratepayers' interests by assuring safe, reliable, and reasonably priced services, while also taking into consideration social and environmental impacts. You write expert testimony and defend it on the witness stand. The goal is fair, equitable rates."

Sam leaned back into his chair and inhaled a whiff of dirty dish rag mixed with frying oil. At least he mentioned fairness and equity, Sam thought.

After a pause, Charlie said, "We don't take sides, and we don't go to war with the company. They are not the enemy. On paper, we're neutral. In reality, we work with them to achieve our goals." Now Sam was exhaling that same dirty air. He could hear someone in the kitchen shouting a curse word. Probably a pile-up of orders. At least it's a job, he thought—anything that sweeps me away from this breakroom has to be an improvement.

When he hung up the phone, Sam shouted "yes!" to the chipped linoleum walls and empty chairs. On his way out he went to the kitchen and found his closest work friend, Jorge, whose forehead was dripping with sweat. Sam gave him three hearty pats on the back. "I'm getting out of here. I got a job."

Before Jorge could answer, Sam was out the door, coat slung over his shoulder. As he raced to the subway, he was overcome with that familiar sinking and floating feeling, like his feet had never been planted on the ground in the first place, like it had always been so.

Chapter 2

It finally happened seventy-five miles from Springfield. A steady knocking, followed by a loud boom that shook the entire car. Then, in the middle of the highway, the vehicle lost its ability to travel the speed limit, in half a second slowing to a crawl. Sam pressed the gas to the floor and jerked the wheel to the right, and the car reached the shoulder as an SUV tore past.

A cop ticketed Sam for an expired registration before calling a tow truck. Sam and his vehicle were dropped at a small repair shop next to a gas station and grocery store—seemingly the only buildings in that town. An enormous man with a grey shirt and hair hardened with gel lowered Sam's car and rolled it into the garage. After fifteen minutes of looking under the hood, the man said, with a shred of sympathy, it would be $2,000 to fix it. "But we'll buy it from you for $300."

Sam looked in the backseat, where all his possessions were piled, mostly books in boxes and clothes hastily thrown into garbage bags. "I need to get to Springfield today."

"I can take you there for fifty bucks," said the mechanic. Sam sighed and threw up his hands.

The mechanic tapped the steering wheel to the rapid drumbeat of a black-metal band Sam didn't recognize as the fields darkened and clouds turned peach and ashy blue. When that radio station grew faint, he started flipping through others. Sam heard a woman's husky voice break through a wall of static. "Our grief is not a cry for war. That's what thousands—no, millions— have been chanting. If you knew what it was like out there—the arrests, the beatings. It's their wars, but it's our dead, goddamnit. Their wars—" Her voice was swallowed by white noise. Sam wanted to ask what spunky small-town community radio station they had just driven past, but the man seemed to like his silence.

When they pulled into Springfield, Sam saw a modest-looking motel about fifty yards from the raised earth of train tracks. "That place is as good as any."

Up close, the motel was more rundown than it had initially appeared. The vinyl siding was marred with cracks and the neon sign that read "Capitol Lodge" was missing three light bulbs. But when the clerk offered a weekly rate of $200, Sam agreed. The room had an unidentifiable sweet smell mixed with cigarette smoke, but there was a shower and a bed—and Sam was exhausted. After toweling off, he lay down, pulled the polyester blanket around his ears, and tried to focus on the sound of his own breath. But his heart pounded and eyes flitted across the dark room. What if I fail? What if I can't do this?

Sam had just nodded off when he heard heavy pounding and felt the floor and walls shake. He saw the road, felt his hands on the wheel, and was seized with the realization that he had just seconds before oncoming traffic crashed into him. But then he heard the whistle of a train—a single, unending note. He gripped his pillow and pulled it over his head, remembering where he was.

***

The next morning, on the edge of downtown, Sam wandered along a side street with small houses and well-manicured lawns, one still bearing a dark-blue Bush/Cheney yard sign from two years ago. A few doors down he saw a light-green two-flat with a homemade sign on the lawn that read, "Apartment for rent." Couldn't hurt to try, he thought.

The door was answered by a short and squat old woman who had dyed maroon hair and smelled faintly of burnt sausage. She smiled broadly and grabbed Sam by the wrist, pulling him through a hallway, up a flight of stairs to the second-floor apartment. Opening the unlocked door, she implored in a thick German accent, "Vhat do you zink?"

It was spacious and bright with big windows on all sides— and furnished with a couch, kitchen table and chairs and even a bed. The place was only $300 a month, half of what he'd paid in his old neighborhood in Chicago. "I think it's pretty nice."

"Vould you like to come live vith Gertrude, yes?" She was still gripping Sam's wrist.

Sam nodded his head rapidly, wondering how likely it was that Gertrude would run a credit check.

"Good, good!" said Gertrude, finally letting go. They agreed Sam would return in a week with all of his things, or at least Sam hoped that's what they'd agreed to. When he asked her about a lease, she replied, "Yes yes, fine fine," then pushed him towards the door, her hand on his back.

As Sam bounded down the steps then out the door, he was

seized with vertigo—the sensation that he couldn't tell whether he was upright, whether he was in the air or on the ground. At the bottom of the steps he paused, felt his feet on the concrete, his heart pounding in his chest. He crossed his arms, almost hugging himself, and walked this way until he was far enough down the street to be out of Gertrude's view. He sat down on a curb and rested his elbows on his knees for a few minutes before flipping open his phone. "Mom, I've got some news."

***

Sam took a deep breath and walked into the lobby. He wore the same suit he had to his interview, but he'd changed his tie. He could still taste the sour residue of the pale brown coffee at the diner. "What can I do for you?" the security guard asked, giving no sign of recognition. The guard, heavy-set with buzzed black hair and silver-rimmed glasses, made a phone call followed by an inexplicable ten seconds looking at a sign-in sheet, then waved Sam through. Sam got on the elevator and, when two others joined him, he straightened his back and nodded in their direction as though he'd done it 1,000 times before. He was now an Office Coworker, and nodding on elevators seemed like something Office Coworkers did.

On the fourth floor, Sam found Dee Dee at her desk talking on her phone. She looked up, throwing Sam a polite but patronizing smile. "Got to go, hon," she said into the receiver. "I'll call you later."

"It looks like you made it," Dee Dee said, glancing up from her chair.

"All in one piece."

Dee Dee pivoted to her computer, and her face disappeared behind a beige monitor, but Sam could see her hand manipulating the mouse. He shifted his weight from foot to foot, until half a minute went by. "Could you let Charlie know I'm here?"

"Charlie? Oh, he's not here yet. He had a small problem at home, but he should be here any minute." After twenty more seconds of scrolling, "You know what, let me show you to your office."

They walked down a hallway with dirty tan walls and a discolored gray carpet. Halfway to the end, Dee Dee ducked into an office and Sam followed. The interior had the same walls and carpet, but at least two big windows let in plenty of sunshine.

"I'll have Charlie come see you as soon as he gets in. Have fun!" Dee Dee was out the door.

Sam looked around. There was a computer, phone, desk, and credenza along with two file cabinets. Sam turned on the computer but could not get beyond a welcome screen requesting a username and password. He rummaged through the desk, found a pen and paper, and started writing a to-do list to pass the time: groceries, book store, ear plugs.

A minute later, Dee Dee reappeared in his office with a large bundle of folders, which she set on his desk with a thump. "To get started, why don't you start going through this testimony?"

Before Sam could ask a question, she was out the door, her footsteps pattering down the carpet covering the hallway.

Sam stared at the folders for a minute. He'd done his homework before starting this position. Companies submit their own "testimony" in question-and-answer format, usually proposing one form of gouging or another, but presented in neutered legalese, like "recovering revenue through a higher customer charge."

And then other "stakeholders," like the Attorney General and the Citizens Utility Board, file their own testimony, as do Commerce Commission staff, who are supposed to describe what the utility is proposing and why or why not the proposal is valid. This endless stream of questions and answers then grows longer as parties submit rebuttals, and then rebuttals to rebuttals. That tall stack then becomes the case, which goes to the administrative law judge for hearings, and then to the five governor-appointed Commissioners. While parties can still appeal their decision, given the pro-utility lean of the commission, it's more like a boring, drawn-out list of concessions, a shakedown with a Master's degree.

Before he could get into a rhythm there was a knock at his door. A short and slight man with straight, thinning brown hair and a matching mustache halted in the doorway. Sam looked closer and saw intelligent eyes peering out of oval, wire-rimmed glasses. "Let me guess," the man said with an apologetic smile, "they have you reading testimony."

"They do this to everyone?" asked Sam.

"I read old testimony for three weeks straight before they threw me into my first case." Sam wanted to respond with a sarcastic comment, but he held back, sensing this man was skittish, that it had taken all his courage to come say hello. "Well, I just wanted to welcome you aboard," the man said, handing Sam a business card with his contact information. "I'm two doors down if you need anything. Name's Greg Caldwell." Sam watched him leave, thinking there was something in his manner that he trusted. The small kindness left him with a pang. I didn't realize how lonely I was, he thought. He put the card in his pocket.

After five minutes passed, Sam walked back down the hallway to see if he could get any instructions about what he was supposed to do with the testimony. Dee Dee was not at her desk, but the light was on in Charlie's office. Sam went in to find his boss reading a newspaper.

"Hey! Dee Dee told me you were here. I meant to stop on by but work caught up with me." Sam looked down to see that Charlie was reading the sports section. "Who's your team?" said Sam.

"Cardinals are my life. You'll learn that about me," Charlie said, gesturing towards a framed and signed Cardinals jersey next to a picture of a pitcher throwing a ball headlined, "Matt Morris." Matt Morris—what a great, corn-fed generic sports name, Sam thought. Of course Charlie's a fan.

"That's really cool." Sam did his best to be impressed.

"Yeah, they blew it in the NLCS, but he was a stud in game five. Gave all he could." Charlie looked back over at Sam. "Who's your team?"

"If I told you the Yankees you'd probably put my office in the boiler room, so I'll say Mets."

"Good answer. You'll learn around here that avoiding unnecessary controversy will get you pretty far. By the way, sorry about the relocation fee. I really did try and get you one. But we do have this for you—figured we'd make up for that by giving it to you a bit early."

Sam gingerly picked up the envelope Charlie had thrust toward him, but was too nervous to inspect it. "Oh, everything's fine. I'm excited to get star—"

"Hey Dee Dee, are you back yet?" Charlie yelled. "Can you find some testimony for Sam to read? That will give him an idea of what we do around here."

"Already did it."

Sam turned to Charlie. "What do you want me to—"

"Just read. Time to get your feet wet." Sam stopped himself from asking a follow-up question when he saw Charlie hold the sports section in front of him, eclipsing the bottom half of his face.

Once in the hallway, Sam opened the envelope, which crinkled loudly in the empty office. He searched the pale blue cardstock for the dollar amount. When he saw $1,344.49, he took a deep breath, thinking that it had been a while since he'd inhaled that much oxygen at once. Sam practically skipped the rest of the way.

When Sam got back to his office, he reached for the top folder and squinted at the first page. Sam couldn't always get his mind to focus when he wanted it to—his thoughts had a way of drifting and circling. In college, he sometimes startled in the middle of a chemistry lecture, realizing he hadn't absorbed a single thing the professor had said. But he never had this problem staring at the faded pages of labor history books. Sometimes he'd stay up all night to prepare for his socialist reading group, something he'd never do for his coursework. "You've got an active mind," his mother had been telling him since he was a kid, "but you have to learn to discipline your thoughts. We have a tendency to make ourselves miserable."

He hadn't seen writing this bland and technical in years. "The purpose of my rebuttal testimony is to report the results of my review of United Gas rebuttal testimony concerning the reconciliation of its Gas Therm Adjustment (GTA) Rider." Sam's eyelids felt like they were made of lead—he had to read each sentence two or three times as he acclimated himself to the jargon, and he was only on the relatively simple witness identification phase. His old curmudgeonly, lefty supervisor at the economic consulting firm thought companies and state regulators made the process intentionally obtuse, because if the public understood what was happening, they'd riot. "The ability to explain complex concepts in clear terms is revolutionary," she told him once.

Sam was startled by a voice. "Lunch is from noon to one," said Dee Dee, popping her head into his office. Sam walked to a corner store a block away and paid for a Diet Coke and a bag of Fritos then carried them back to the office, not wanting to be the last to return from break.

When he returned to the fourth floor, the hallway was empty. He sat down at his desk and wiped the grease from his fingers. After a while, his reading began to pick up pace. Sam remembered that he could understand the language of testimony, although he'd always approached it from the advocacy side. It was quite simple, really. United Gas wanted to hike—or as they call it, "restructure"—customer rates over the next four years to "smooth out" the company's revenue, as an insurance policy against possible future losses in the event rate-payers purchased less gas. But if these possible losses never came to bear, the company would not have to pay back the excess charges, making it a win-win for the company.

What bullshit, thought Sam. He was under no illusions about his job—he wasn't ushering in a thousand years of emancipatory egalitarianism for the masses, but he could still provide a small cushion for the consumer, a veneer of protection. I've got to talk to Charlie about this, he thought to himself, show him I'm not fooled by the company's transparent arguments.

He raced down the hallway, but the light to Charlie's office was out.

"He had to leave early," Dee explained from behind her computer. "His son is in a football tournament. Star player."

"I guess Charlie needed to take a break from all that overtime he's been racking up," said Sam, angling for a laugh. Dee Dee gave him a quizzical look. "Is there a schedule of when he's in I can reference so I can plan a bit better?"

Dee Dee let out a faint grin. "Four months, two months, six months."

Sam stared back, perplexed. "This a riddle?"

"That's how long the last three people who had your job stayed, hon. Everyone else here stays for years, even decades, but the junior rate analysts for Charlie—they come and go like head colds. Now this may sound scary to you, but I promise, it's not. It's an entry level position. You work a few months, a year, then you move on, usually to the private sector. But the one thing they all have in common—"

"The people who came before?"

"The boys who had your job, yes. The one thing they had in common is they learned to go at a certain pace, a certain demeanor. There's a rhythm to the office, Sam."

"Right."

"You don't wear worried well, sweetie. You're too young. United ain't going anywhere. Charlie will be in when he's in and you can hash things out then, okay?"

"Of course, thank you." Sam headed back to his office to read over more United files. Even if everyone else cut out early, he wasn't going to. But as he sat in his chair, he couldn't get his eyes to focus on the fine print. Such a quick turnover for his position. Was Charlie a hair-trigger boss, quick to fire? Or was it really that juicy of an entry role? Sam thought about the belongings he'd just schlepped from Chicago to Springfield, and the long odds he could afford a move back—or anywhere.

Chapter 3

The first thing Sam noticed about her was that she had an honest face: brown eyes with brows slanted downwards towards her cheekbones, touched with a light rouge, her large nose peppered with light brown freckles, wavy chestnut hair that cascaded to her shoulders. She wore a navy-blue pantsuit that clung to her lithe frame, but Sam could picture her in a t-shirt and jeans at the farmer's market, carefully examining beets before placing them in a canvas tote slung from her shoulder. She was the only woman at the energy conservation meeting, on the fourth floor of the attorney general's office, and she sat at the far corner of the conference table.

Sam held a notepad and pen on his lap, unsure of what he was doing here. Just minutes ago, Charlie had come into Sam's office, for the first time since Sam had started at the Commission, and told him, "Hey, I've got a family emergency at home and have to cut out. Could you cover a three o'clock meeting?"

Of course Sam said yes. All he'd done since he started five days ago was pore over old testimony, and he was eager to get a sense of what might exist beyond the confines of his office. He'd taken to keeping his door shut to avoid the lobbyists and utility reps who freely roamed the halls—recognizable as a cut above the rest: smoother skin, more meticulous haircuts, bodies chiseled by hours at the gym.

Feeling like he had just emerged from a cave, Sam squinted as the mid-afternoon sun poured through a long vertical window to his left, illuminating a column of dust suspended in air above the table. He didn't recognize anyone.

After a couple of minutes, a middle-aged man with curly hair atop an enormous head said, "Who are we waiting for?"

Two older men rushed in. The first was bald and unkempt in a wrinkled shirt, the second was tall with wavy black hair, wearing a crisply ironed white shirt with gold cufflinks.

The large-headed man started in, "Hi folks. We have a busy agenda here so everybody should try to stay on point. Oh, before we get started, this guy over here is Sam Golden, Charlie's new analyst. It seems that Charlie had some important family business to attend to."

"Yeah, sure!" a man said under his breath—Sam didn't catch who.

Sam learned that this large-headed man was Bill Arnold, the Commissioner appointed by the governor and confirmed by the Senate to oversee the Public Utilities Division. "You're all aware that the legislature has passed a law requiring utilities to offer their customers energy conservation programs subject to approval by the Commission," Bill said. "So, let's take the opportunity to kick around some ideas on the kind of process we want to establish to review and analyze these programs. Yes, Jerry?"

The unkempt man said, "You know this law is total bullshit. It's just another excuse for the utility to jack up rates to deal with the phony issue of global warming. Why are we wasting time on this?"

"Why?" the man with cufflinks cut in. "Because the legislature told us we had to. So, now you're wasting *our* time, Jerry."

"Michael, when did you become such a wimp?" Jerry shot back.

"Fellas, fellas, let's focus here. Any thoughts on the process?"

Twenty minutes of desultory discussion followed. Sam gathered that the cost of insulating individual residences would be used to justify higher rates, so companies would once again pass the cost of carbon emissions onto the public while giving lip service to environmentalism. Even still, the plan was opposed by more than half the room over concerns it was unduly burdensome to utilities. They wanted to know how it could be mitigated—whether there was a workaround. What a pointless debate, thought Sam, who briefly let his eyes wander to the other corner of the room. The woman gave him a brief nod and mouthed the word "welcome," her eyebrows arched. Sam knew it was too much to hope for, but he wondered if it was possible that she was as disgusted with these proceedings as he was—that she was drawing him into an inside joke. There seemed to be a feisty intelligence about her, or maybe Sam was just lonely and projecting. He pressed a smile into his palm.

Bill said, "Let me take a moment to summarize—"

Before he could finish the sentence, Michael jumped up. "Got to take a conference call. Do whatever the hell you want with this." He dashed out.

"Thank God he's gone!" said Jerry.

Bill's attempt to summarize the discussion communicated nothing: He'd take everyone's concerns into consideration, he was meeting with the Democratic speaker of the Illinois House next week, and everyone would be hearing from him soon.

27

The room began buzzing with conversation, but Bill shushed them. "We're not done. I have one more important matter." Once everyone was quiet Bill stood up from his chair, hands on his hips. "You're to treat this with the strictest confidence. We've received word from our partners in business and law enforcement that a journalist who's been seeking to gain confidential information about our critical infrastructure networks could constitute a security threat, whether intentionally or not." Bill lowered his voice as though the security breach were right outside the door. "If anyone is contacted by a journalist, please let me know immediately. No exceptions."

Sam felt a pressure between his temples. Partners in business and law enforcement? That sounded pretty vague. As the murmur of conversation picked back up, Sam gathered up his coat and notebook. He didn't muster the courage to glance at her again before leaving.

***

Hours later, while working in his office, Sam met the tall born-again woman he'd frequently seen roaming the halls but mostly avoided. Julie was north of fifty, her brunette hair cut in a clean bob, and she wore Jesus like a perfume. Sam wasn't hostile to this per se, only to too much talking, which usually went along with that brand of affectation.

She appeared in his open doorway, chewing gum. "Knock, knock!" she yelled, while pretending to knock on the door.

Sam looked up from the testimony he was reading—his third time trying to comprehend the argument of a witness named Robert Gentile. Before Sam could speak, she bounded inside and plopped down in an empty chair.

"My name is Julie, but you can call me Julie!" she said and broke out into a guffaw. "I have been working here for thirty-three years and I plan to retire in exactly one year, six months, and three days. What do you think of that?"

"I think you are a very lucky person."

"I come from Johnstown. I bet you have no idea where that is."

Sam said nothing.

"Well, it is a special place fifty miles west of here. The most beautiful place on the planet! And my father is a very important person there. Did I mention that he is a great golfer? I mean he's seventy-four years old and still drives the ball 250 yards."

"If Johnstown is so special, why did you move here?"

"Oh, I would never leave Johnstown."

"So you drive fifty miles each way back and forth to work every day?"

"You betcha!"

"Isn't that boring?"

"Oh no! I love my time in the car. I spend all my time listening to Bible verses. Can you even imagine? It is such a special time for me!"

Sam couldn't think of what to say to that, but it didn't matter. Julie told him about her pet dog (would've won first place in a dog show if she had shown him), her recent visit to Las Vegas, her daughter's new boyfriend (needs to learn his manners).

Sam picked up a pen and pulled the cap on and off. He pictured the men from the Commission meeting gathered around the conference table, the woman in the corner, who seemed detached from the room, floating above it. Why had there been so much debate about an essentially toothless energy conservation policy? he wondered.

Julie stood up and walked over to the doorway, still talking. Sam came to and realized she was blocking his only path of escape. This was the second time today he felt the urge to bolt from the room.

"I hate to interrupt, but I'm late for a meeting," Sam blurted.

Julie raised her eyebrows and chewed her gum three times before asking, "What's the meeting about?"

"I have to talk about a case."

"What case? I don't think there's a meeting scheduled at all today."

"Sorry, I'm too late to talk. Nice to meet you!" Sam rushed out of his door and down the hallway, realizing he had to fully commit to his story. He pressed the button for the fifth floor.

This floor looked remarkably similar to the fourth, except where Dee Dee's rounded desk would have been, there was nothing.

Sam turned left and noticed a door slightly ajar. The lights were off and Sam could glimpse one end of an oak table and three empty chairs surrounding it. An empty conference room.

Sam walked in, and before he oriented himself, realized this was not a room he belonged in. Four men were gathered around the other end of the table—the side you couldn't see from the hallway. "Oh, sorry, I thought this room was empty."

The men stopped talking and looked at him in unison.

"Oh, it's just my new analyst," said a perturbed voice. Sam looked closer. It was Charlie.

"This meeting's not for you, son. What are you doing wandering around this floor, anyway?"

"I was, um, confused about where I was."

The man to Charlie's left stood up. He was tall and slender, hair swept back away from his forehead, wearing a form-fitting black suit. He put his left hand on Sam's back, still clutching a white binder in his right, and guided him to the door. "Not a problem."

As Sam walked out, he looked back at the man and glanced at his binder. In big black lettering it said "InfraGard." And beneath that, in smaller print, "FBI Anti-Terror National Infrastructure Center."

Strange, thought Sam, as he speedwalked back to the elevator. What could the FBI want with a commerce commission in a two-bit town like this? Sam pressed the button for the fourth floor and waited, facing the wall.

He heard faint footsteps, and the sound of something being dragged or pulled towards him.

Sam turned around. Angelo.

"What are you doing here?" said Angelo. "Hanging out with the big shots?"

"Actually, I was lost. And then they told me to get lost."

Sam held out his hand and Angelo grabbed it, giving it a firm shake. His hand was warm, and Sam was surprised at how relieved he felt to see Angelo, even if he had a penchant for running into Sam just as he was fumbling to fit into this place.

"Looks like you got the job. Sam, is it?"

"Yes and yes, for now. Not sure how much I'm *in* in though. Having a hard time parsing dislike from indifference."

"They invite you to the football pool yet?"

"No. Shit, is that bad?"

"Sam."

"Yeah?"

"There is no football pool. I'm just messin' with you. You'll be fine." Angelo patted him on the back as he pushed past him. "Just watch what rooms you walk into."

"You got it."

When he reached the fourth floor, Sam had already moved on to the immediate task of dodging Julie—who still had several of her daughter's terriers' names to list off—before reaching his office and shutting his door behind him. If Springfield, Illinois was a target worthy of al Qaeda, he thought to himself, they really needed to realign their priorities.

Chapter 4

The next morning, Sam checked out of the motel.

"Aw, are you kidding me," the cab driver said when he realized he'd been dispatched to help some guy move. Sam could hear the throaty wailing and heavy drumbeat of Creed emanating from the radio.

"You don't have to lift a finger, I'll do it all myself," said Sam, quickly tossing the boxes and bags into the backseat until it was impossible to see out of the rearview mirror. Sam could be sloppy, but he took pride in his speed and scrappiness.

On the ride there the jittery cab hit a bump, a box tipped over, and out fell an old pin: "Save the Stamford Press-Times." His uncle had given it to him when he was fifteen, when his union was fighting hard for survival against newsroom "consolidations." Their efforts failed and his Uncle Larry, a brilliant journalist and Sam's personal hero, was left bagging groceries in his late 60s. One can never pinpoint the exact moment when radical politics becomes the lens through which one sees the world, but watching those arthritic fingers try and peel the thin plastic bags apart when they should have been typing away about some political misdeed was a major one. "Unionism is simply mechanized empathy," he'd once told Sam.

Sam gave the front door a couple of raps. Gertrude immediately appeared. "Vhere have you been? Vhere have you been?"

They walked up the stairs, Sam gripping two bags in each hand, and Gertrude opened the door without a key. She lingered while Sam put his clothes in the far corner of the living room. About to head back down to grab the rest of his things, Sam extended his palm toward Gertrude. "The key?"

"Oh, the key, the key!"

She reached into her pocket, pulled out a key and said, "Zhis is for ze front door."

"How about the key for my apartment?"

"You are safe here. I vill vatch. I vill make sure no one comes in."

Sam lifted his eyebrows and rolled his eyes—the same look of incredulity he could picture his mother giving him if he relayed this story to her.

Sam shrugged and exhaled. "Sure, why not?" he said. "What could possibly go wrong?"

***

By now, Sam had grown accustomed to the light in Charlie's office often being off, Dee Dee talking on her phone, his coworkers wandering the hallways doing office visits—sometimes for hours.

It was clear Julie preferred other coworkers to Sam. Her two favorites, John and Jack, were both around her age. John was slim with small, delicate hands and a booming voice. Jack was heavy-set, his forehead often sprinkled with small beads of sweat. He was more soft-spoken, except when he got riled up. Then he turned bright red, and his vocal range would jump.

The next Monday, on his way to the bathroom, Sam was obstructed by the three of them standing in the hallway just outside his office door. Jack was unleashing epithets about a parking ticket he had unfairly received. "I'm sure I parked at least fifteen feet away from the goddamn hydrant! Besides, if I was a foot or two too close, what is the big fucking deal? I mean you have gangbangers doing what the hell ever they feel like in this town and the cops have nothing better to do than get out their tape measures because my car might have been a couple of inches too close. Really?"

"You know, the same thing happened to my daddy," Julie piped up. "A Johnstown cop made the mistake of giving him a ticket for speeding in a school zone. Well, the police chief lives on daddy's street and when he found out, he personally ripped that ticket up the very next day!"

"I mean we have gangbangers running wild in this town!" said Jack. "And they come after me?" Jack caught sight of Sam, who'd been doing his best to skulk past the conversation unnoticed. "What do you think, new guy?"

"What do I think?" Sam repeated hoping that repeating the question would be enough to satisfy Jack.

It wasn't. "Yes, what do you think?"

Sam looked from Julie to John to Jack, who still had fire in his eyes.

He remembered his bar mitzvah when he'd made an entire room of people roar with laughter at the expense of the rabbi, an ill-humored man, who had prepared a sermon on the theme that one grows in "size," but also in "sighs"—that is, physically, as well as emotionally. To drive home his point, the rabbi had turned to Sam and said, "Your suit is a good size, right?" Sam replied, "No, it doesn't fit." By the rabbi's fifth failed attempt to get Sam to play along with the pun, which thirteen-year-old Sam found droll and stupid, his mother was giggling into her handkerchief, his brother was letting out a belly laugh. Afterwards, Sam's mother had scolded him. "You completely screwed up the rabbi's speech."

"But you were laughing," he'd said.

"That doesn't matter," she'd replied. "There's no excuse for being cruel."

Sam looked again at Jack, his face expectant. Thirty-two years old, and he was still working on not being cruel. Suddenly, he heard a shrill ring come from his office. It took Sam a moment to realize this was a call—no one had phoned his line since he'd started.

"Sorry, gotta run." He rushed in and closed the door behind him.

"Hi, this is Greg down the hall. I saw that the triple J's had you cornered so I thought you might need an excuse to get away."

"Triple J's, they like a Doo-Wop band?"

"No one's ever seen them apart from each other. They roam the halls looking for weak game," said Greg.

Sam gave a closed-mouth laugh. Finally, a co-conspirator.

"I'll be on the lookout."

***

The saccharin odor of vanilla-bean air freshener filled Sam's nostrils, and he thought he might be sick. Sam wanted to roll down the passenger-side window, but it was too cold outside, and besides, this wasn't his car. Dee Dee had been kind enough to drive him to a meeting for One Springfield, a tenants' organization that had requested someone from the Commerce Commission attend their meeting.

He'd been doing an admirable job at avoiding the Triple J's, but doubly so Julie, who greeted him in the early hours every single day with a cheerful, "Blessed day." No matter where he entered, or what time, she was there with a hearty "blessed day," a Christian T-1000 seeking out the office Jew and reminding him of the good word. He knew she meant no malice by it, and mostly it bothered him because he never knew how to respond. He usually just stammered out a "You too?" before she bustled away.

Just twenty minutes earlier, on his way back from the bathroom, Jack had called him into his office where he'd found him, Julie, and John having one of their endless afternoon conversations. "Hey, new guy, mind covering for me and going to this bullshit community meeting?" Sam figured this sounded better than combing through old testimony, so he agreed, and now here he was in a car that smelled like it could kill invasive weeds.

"It's not safe to come to the East Side at night time," said Dee Dee.

"Where is the East Side?"

37

"We're there, hon. Once you cross the 10th Street railroad tracks."

"Literally the other side of the tracks?"

"The expression came from somewhere, I s'ppose."

The street they were driving down didn't look that different from the one Sam lived on. Except, instead of sidewalks, there was just overgrown grass that reached all the way to the road. They passed an empty lot where piles of beer bottles, soda cans, and shoes were interspersed with three-foot-tall weeds. About 100 feet down, half of a roof had collapsed, yet a light still shone through the window. Sam felt his seatbelt pull taut as the car's right tire hit a pothole. Okay, maybe the East Side was different.

"Oh, I'm not coming in," Dee Dee said when they arrived. "You have fun!"

The church was made of brick and shaped like a perfect rectangle, nothing remarkable about its exterior other than that it was ringed by a large parking lot and, unlike the surrounding houses, had sidewalks and a mowed lawn. Sam had gotten over his allergy to churches during his college years, when a rent control campaign had him going to a musty church basement every week for coalition meetings.

He pushed open the large oak door and walked left into a sparsely furnished room, where eight women were seated on folding chairs arranged in a small circle, with no table at the center. Seven black women, most of them elders, all wearing red shirts, and a younger white woman with chin-length shag hair the color of sawdust, wearing thick black glasses, dressed in what could only be described as frumpy business casual. "Hello, who are you?" asked a woman who seemed about fifty.

"Sam Golden. I'm the new guy at the Commerce Commission."

"Well, no one's perfect," said an old woman sitting at the point of the circle farthest from where Sam was standing, her white hair cropped close to her head.

"We're so glad you could make it," said the fifty-ish woman as she carried over another folding chair and motioned for Sam to sit down to her right, joining the circle. "The Commission hardly ever comes to these meetings. We were in the middle of discussing how United jacked up their prices. We invited you because we know they're trying to raise prices more."

"Oh, I didn't—"

"Mrs. Belinda was telling us about how the increases affected her." The young woman pointed to the woman with white close-cropped hair, and he took a closer look at her. She was wearing bright red lipstick, which she had clearly dabbed on her cheeks as rouge, and a turquoise beaded necklace hanging down to her belly. Mrs. Belinda held Sam's gaze.

"Do you know what it's like to choose between heat and medicine?"

Sam thought about the medical bills that were almost certainly piling up at his old apartment, about the clean bill of health—and unshakable debt—he'd received after his $8,000 MRI. "Not technically, no, but—"

"My husband died three years ago, and now I'm on one fixed income. I'm in no shape to get a job, even though I'm still smart as a whip—and gorgeous too."

Sam laughed.

"So when United raises my heat bill once, and then again,

something's got to give. I have an enlarged heart. Do you know what that is, son? I'll give you a clue: It doesn't mean I'm a nice person."

Mrs. Belinda paused to catch her breath. "It means I need to take pills to keep my blood pumping. Last winter was freezing and I couldn't afford my bill. I tried turning off the heat and cranking my oven to high, keeping all the burners on, all my doors shut." She rubbed her hands together, mimicking the act of attempting to warm herself. "But after a day huddling by my oven, I realized it was too cold. My back ached, every muscle tense. It wasn't going to work. So for two months, I cut my pills by a quarter so I could pay."

Sam looked around the room and realized everyone was watching him, waiting for him to say something. Half of the people there looked like they were older than seventy. Sam noticed for the first time the text on their shirts, "One Springfield," in front of an image of the state capitol building.

The young woman in frumpy business casual sat across from him, to Mrs. Belinda's left, and was watching him intently. She wore a grey sweater, a white collared shirt underneath, beige slacks.

"What about Illinois Cares?" asked Sam. "They're supposed to subsidize low-income people who are unable to pay." Sam rotated ninety degrees in his chair so that he was looking straight at Mrs. Belinda.

The young woman cut in so loudly it made Sam start. Her voice sounded too raspy for her years. "They were cut out of the Illinois budget and ran out of money last December," she said.

"There's also a delayed payment program—"

"Still waiting to hear back." Mrs. Belinda added. "It took me weeks to figure out how to fill out that paperwork after my husband died. He used to take care of those things. The cold moves faster than the mail does, and I don't have a computer. So I had to choose."

The young woman jumped in, impatiently pushing her hair out of her eyes as she spoke. "This is a common problem. We see it across Sangamon County. Not having the access or information to apply to those programs is the equivalent of not having those programs at all. Which I'm sure does not escape the utilities that design them this way. But, what am I saying—this is your field, not mine."

"Excuse me, what is your field?" Sam said to the young woman.

Just then, Sam's phone rang. A Springfield number. "I'm so sorry, but I need to get this."

Sam ran into the hallway. "Yes?"

"Sam, it's Charlie. Don't tell me you actually went to that One Springfield meeting."

"I'm here now."

"Aw, we were just messing with you. One Springfield invites us to every poorly attended potluck and sob fest they put on. We usually stay far away. You should have checked with me first, you stupid son of a bitch."

"Actually, there's some interesting stuff here, I think I might—"

"You gotta get here now. My ass is on the line. There's an important gala for the Healthy Futures Alliance. I need you here, man. Big dick suits wanna meet the new guy."

"Uh, I'd rather stay."

"Dee Dee's already on her way. I called her, told her this was a prank. Apparently she didn't get the memo either."

Sam walked back into the room where One Springfield was gathered and stood outside the circle, behind his empty chair.

"Something came up, I assume?" said Mrs. Belinda.

"I…"

"This was a record for y'all."

Another woman jumped in. "We appreciate your coming."

"Let me guess, it's that scholarship award ceremony," said Mrs. Belinda.

"The what? I'm sorry, I don't actually know what it's about. I've only been in this role a week."

"Well good luck to that kid. He'll need it. I know half a dozen students who never even got their scholarship."

Sam thought it was an odd thing to say but needed to run, he could hear Dee Dee's horn from the parking lot. "Thank you so much for having me. I really have to go." Sam felt sheepish.

Mrs. Belinda said nothing. The echo of Sam's footsteps seemed cartoonishly loud as he walked out of the room.

Just as he was pushing the door to step outside, Sam felt a tap on his shoulder and quickly spun around. It was the young woman with dark glasses.

"Sorry, I wasn't trying to be an asshole," she said, her tone indicating she wasn't sorry at all. "It's just that I've never seen the Commerce Commission come to one of these meetings. I've been working on a story about United for ten months, and it's been very difficult for anyone to talk to me."

"The thing is, I'm just a nobody, low man on the food chain. Not much I can even tell you."

"Funny, everyone I talk to over there tells me the same thing—seems to be a government building with 500 interns."

Sam saw Dee Dee laying on her horn. "I'm sorry—"

"Will you at least take this?" she said, thrusting a beige card into Sam's hand. Allison O'Donnell, *Springfield Weekly*, it read.

Sam shoved the card into his pocket and got into the car. "Who was that?" asked Dee Dee.

Something inside of Sam warned him against divulging too much. "Just someone from the meeting."

"Huh. She seemed like she was running after you." Dee Dee paused. "That's what they're always like, though. Those organizations are so desperate, it breaks my heart. I truly wish we could do more, but we're just cogs in a machine and it's all on the Legislature anyhow."

"Yeah," said Sam, wondering whether this journalist from a podunk alt-weekly could be the security threat the Commissioner had warned about at the energy conservation meeting. There was no way in hell he was telling the higher ups about Allison's query—he would never be a snitch. Besides, he hadn't even said anything. Sam reached into his pocket and felt the card's edge prick his fingertips.

Testimony

Dee Dee turned the radio to an oldies station as they made their way back to the West Side—past abandoned lots, empty front porches, and the occasional dilapidated corner store. She dropped him off at a six-story brick building with white shutters, not far from the Commerce Commission.

When he walked through the front door, he was immediately hit with the smell of rosemary chicken and the sound of people cheering and clapping. He picked up a brochure from a tall circular table. It trumpeted, "Healthy Futures Scholarship: High Standards, High Achievement." Flipping through it, Sam walked to the back center of the room where he leaned against a tall, rectangular pillar.

"I want you to give yourselves a huge round of applause for being here tonight," said a man, his lustrous cocoa-colored hair swept back into a calculated, wavy shag, faint wrinkles fanning from the corners of his eyes, a dark beard meticulously groomed into straight lines that cut across his ivory complexion.

"That's right, each and every one of you could have been anywhere else this evening, but you decided to be here. Because you believe in community. You believe in youth. I want to hear you give it up—for you!" The man's million-watt smile made Sam think of the youth ministry guys who tabled at his college campus—hip, chiseled, and in on some secret that Sam would never be privy to. Sam hesitated before clapping softly.

Sam began leafing through the brochure. "We give our best to our youth, and we demand nothing but the best from them," it said on the front. On the inside flap, there was a bullet-pointed list of criteria scholarship recipients are required to meet: a 3.9 GPA, a student-in-residence job program, extracurricular activity. Jesus, Sam thought. I would never meet these standards.

The man pointed his microphone at the room, which was divided into about twenty white-draped tables, each seating five

44

or six people. When the crowd erupted into applause, the man touched his hand to his heart, then pressed both palms together in a gesture of gratitude, one hand still holding the mic.

Something about that gesture made Sam lean into the pillar so hard it forced an exhale. He'd seen that movement before. Phil from his old affinity group used to do that when they started off a meeting. A way of saying he was glad to be there. Sam had always found it a bit Heavens Gate-y, or maybe, he'd suspected, aimed at projecting false sensitivity to the woman members of the affinity group. But Sam's eye rolling had always been internal. That was back when he was trying harder to spare people his judgmental observations.

"This scholarship is one of the most generous in the state, and in return we expect the highest standards from our young leaders," said the man. "Now, for our guest of honor. I've known this young gentleman since he started our after-school program three years ago, and I can tell you, he is an inspiration." The man rattled off a resume of hardships: his father is in prison, he spent the first four years of his life in and out of homeless shelters, his cousin, who he grew up with, was killed in a drive-by shooting two years ago.

Sam put his palm to his cheek. It *was* Phil, it had to be, but without the buzzed hair and his typical tight t-shirt emblazoned with some obscure punk band or sanctimonious political slogan. Sam would recognize that cadence anywhere—the combination of confidence and calculated humility he'd heard so many times during hours-long meetings where Phil would always keep his cool. But now it was tinged with something else. It had a layer of sheen on top of it.

Sam hadn't seen Phil since their affinity group had fallen out. He'd expected to be in some touch, but Phil hadn't once tried to contact him. And then when Sam moved on, he'd felt too bad to reach out. He hated to think this about anyone, because it's exactly how the cops sew division on the left, but he couldn't shake the feeling that Phil had been a snitch or infiltrator, or something—and that Phil's sudden departure was simply him completing whatever task he'd been given. But he'd never have said this out loud. Sam knew there's nothing more destructive than snitch-jacketing and he'd always erred on the side of keeping it to himself.

As the room again echoed with applause, a gangly teenager who couldn't have been much older than sixteen shuffled to the front, looking at his feet. He was wearing a dark brown suit, with matching shoes. His closely cropped hair looked meticulously brushed. The teenager gripped the mic and the room went silent.

Sam looked at a table to his left where a thirty-something woman, who was wearing a pink dress with a matching hat, blew the teenager a kiss. Two small children sat to her right.

"I—I am so grateful for this opportunity," he said, his voice cracking. "I'll be the first in my family to go to college." He paused and, as he looked again at the table, a tall, Swedish-looking man in a midnight-blue suit and pointed leather shoes started walking towards the teenager. He was carrying a large, blown-up check.

The man, grinning, handed the check to the teenager then vigorously shook his hand before grabbing the mic. "On behalf of the Healthy Futures board, I'm thrilled to present this young man with the annual 'United for the Future' scholarship. I'm Thomas French, the president of United Gas, and we're humbled to partner on this gift."

Sam couldn't help but think about the Raytheon Co. scholarship he'd read about last week in the *Journal-Register's* local section. The image was similar: a brochure-ready "urban youth" being exploited for feel-good collateral on the cheap. "We believe that children should reach for their dreams, no matter the circumstances of their birth," a senior executive had told the paper. That same day, the Register had run an AP cover story about how Raytheon's stocks are surging thanks to the War on Terror's premium on precision-guided munitions and missile defense systems.

Sam thought of the One Springfield meeting he'd been ordered to leave to come here. The rich love poor people as long as they're gratefully receiving their charity at a white tablecloth event, not angrily demanding what's theirs. What was Phil doing with these people? Sam wondered.

He took a closer look at the teenager's face as the room applauded again—he was unsmiling, watchful.

Thomas French started speaking slowly, each word dripping with sincerity. "We at United Gas believe in giving back to the community. Kids like him are our future. There's nothing they can't do if they work hard and believe in themselves. As long as he keeps spending long nights hitting the books, we'll be working hard to keep his lights on."

The teenager started inching towards the back wall, still holding the large check. As the sound of applause filled the room, Charlie got up from a table and walked towards Sam, narrow shoulders barely filling out his black sports jacket. He softly punched Sam's shoulder. "Running a bit late, huh?"

Sam let out a weak laugh. "Good one, Charlie," he said.

"We do it to all the new guys, they usually catch on before 5 PM. So how was the group therapy session?"

"You been to one?"

"In the early '90s, after the McCaul scandal, some bleeding-heart legislators took charge for about ten minutes. They would force us to go hear these groups out. They even took attendance like it was some court-mandated AA meeting. I assume they're still reading the same list of grievances."

"I suppose. Some things they mentioned, you know—"

"Look Sam, we don't take sides. It's in our charter. We have to stay above the fray, or it compromises our objectivity."

"Is that what we're doing here, being objective?"

Charlie acted like he hadn't heard. "Listen, we saved you a spot at our table." Charlie made two beckoning motions with his hand, and Sam followed. His seat was right next to Thomas French, who had by now abandoned his sincere tone.

"Word of advice," Thomas leaned into Sam's personal space as Charlie sat down. "They over pour the mixers, be sure to ask for liquor neat."

Sam cleared his throat and nodded politely. "Noted. Thanks."

Charlie, who had taken a seat to Sam's left, turned to him. "Hey, you busy tomorrow? I have something I'd like you to do."

"Oh, yeah, sure, I'm free tomorrow. Just reviewing old testimony. What do you need help with?"

"Later. This isn't the time or place to discuss it," whispered Charlie.

A voice boomed behind Sam. "Well if it isn't Sam Golden." Sam whipped around. It was Phil, smiling widely. Up close Sam could see his perfectly shaped eyebrows. They've probably been waxed, Sam thought, as he unconsciously lifted his fingers to the wild tufts of hair between his own brows.

"Don't say you don't know who I am." Phil held his smile, both rows of sparkling white teeth showing, but his eyes were serious—studying Sam's face.

"No way!" Sam exclaimed, feigning like he'd just figured it out.

Phil nodded his head, still smiling, as he raised a hand and gave a single wave.

"You look great," said Sam, and Phil nodded his head, not bothering to return the compliment. "I haven't seen you since—"

"I vanished?" Phil twirled his fingers in the air with a flourish, mimicking a magician.

Phil pulled over a seat and placed himself between Sam and Charlie.

"Wow. How are you?" Sam leaned close, speaking in a loud whisper, not that he could stop Thomas French from overhearing.

"I'm good, man. Really, really good. So much to catch up on. You won't believe it—I'm working for United in the regulatory department."

"I, I—"

"The culture at United, in a lot of companies, has changed over the last few years. They're really trying to give back. And they tap people like me to make that happen. Mackey and Rodgers are calling it Conscious Business."

What was happening? Sam had given up organizing, but he never deluded himself that the other side was good, and that switching over was a virtue. He'd always had doubts about Phil's motives, but this was a plot twist he hadn't seen coming.

He wanted to ask Phil why he'd decided to cross sides, what happened after the affinity group fell apart and they all stopped talking. But he stopped himself, remembering who was sitting to his left.

"Am I supposed to know who 'Mackey and Rodgers' are?"

Phil let out a loud laugh. "That's what I love about you, man. Your sense of humor. Your energy hasn't changed a bit, even if you look... different."

"Different?"

"Scrappy. You look scrappy. It's good, you wear it well. We've got a lot to catch up on, man." Phil's smile began to slowly drop as he leaned forward, resting his elbows on his knees, cheek pressed into his open palm. "So how are you? Tell me everything." He opened his hands in Sam's direction.

"I don't know where to begin. I just star—"

"Actually, I know all about it." Phil spoke with the calm self-assurance of a guru. "I've been rooting for you ever since you applied."

"Oh, uh, thanks."

"In fact, I recommended he hire you." Phil hoisted his drink in the air, his forefinger pointed towards Thomas French.

Sam turned to his left and Thomas French gave Phil a single nod. "It's true, son. This man thought you were the right guy."

Sam wanted to ask why the hell the company would have any say in who gets hired at an ostensibly neutral regulatory agency. But instead, he watched wordlessly as Phil lifted his drink high in the air.

Increasing the volume of his voice, Thomas lifted his wine glass, accepting the volley. "To helping the underprivileged."

"And the scrappy," Phil joined in. "May they be given a chance to succeed."

Chapter 5

The next morning, Sam's eyes ran over testimony of the president of Pilgrim Associates, whose submission was decorated with gaudy company letterhead, the president's entire resume in the left margin—going back all the way to his anthropology degree at the local university. But Sam couldn't seem to absorb the words, he kept looking out the window at the parking lot, his chin resting on his hand as he watched cars pull in. What am I supposed to do for Charlie today? he wondered.

A silver Ford Explorer pulled into the lot and backed into a parking space. Cars around here are so damn big, thought Sam, tanks designed for mountain-side off-roading. But they just haul people over perfectly flat roads, from their suburban homes to work and back. The door opened and Charlie stepped out. Wait, what was he doing here so early? Sam couldn't recall ever seeing him at the office before ten o'clock.

Sam could hear the triple J's outside of his door, which was cracked open.

"Have you noticed how disgusting the bathrooms are lately?" said Jack. "It looks like a bus station bathroom."

"You should see the women's," said Julie.

"The janitor's in a union, which is just permission to be lazy—at the taxpayer's expense, no less," said John.

"Remember when that one lady tried to start one for us way back?" said Julie.

He knew it would come off as an affront, but Sam stood up and closed the door. He heard the Triple J's go silent, and then footsteps wandering down the hallway.

He sat back down and stared at the testimony. Three minutes later, Charlie was stepping through Sam's door.

"Come with me."

Sam grabbed a notebook and his coat, and the two walked to the elevator, Charlie nodding to Dee Dee as they passed her desk. She gave a quick smile, her phone pressed to her ear.

"I see you're working hard," Charlie said as the elevator slowly descended to the first floor. "We like to throw people into the fire, make them figure it out for themselves. It builds character, toughens you up. That's what I did." Charlie's voice perked up. He must somehow believe what he's saying, Sam sneered to himself.

Sam followed Charlie through the hallway and out the door, where a Ford Explorer was waiting, this one black and shiny. Sam jumped in, Charlie gave the roof two whacks, and the car drove off.

Sam fidgeted with his seatbelt before looking up. The man behind the wheel had the paunch of a former high school football player, with wide shoulders, a thick neck, and light blond hair buzzed into a crew cut so tight the sides and back faded into pure scalp. There was someone in the passenger's seat in front of Sam. He saw a head of wavy brunette hair moving as the person turned around to face him.

Sam felt his blood rush to his chest. The woman from the energy conservation meeting.

"Here is your mission, should you choose to accept it," she said in a husky voice, holding a grave expression for a few seconds before her face crumpled into high-pitched laughter. "Seriously though, has anyone told you what we're doing today?"

"Totally in the dark. Also, hi, I'm Sam." He could feel his pulse drumming in his temples and wondered if it was visible beneath his head of curls, which were more subdued in the dry weather.

"Wendy. I work on the other side of the fourth floor, assistant to our fearless leader Charlie." Sam was surprised by her acerbic tone and confident smile.

"I'm Keith Landrey from inspections. I mostly do gas lines. You're both helping me on a very important task today." He spoke in a crisp, rural Missouri drawl, his voice higher-pitched than Sam was expecting.

Dark layers of clouds blanketed the sun, which looked like a small, silvery pool reflecting some other source of light. Outside the window, the wind sent dry leaves spiraling up then crashing back to the sidewalk. Downtown Springfield looked like a ghost town, with old-timey signs advertising popcorn, fudge, North Star Bar, gag gifts for holiday pranksters, but no one outside. The car pulled up to a stop sign and Keith turned around.

"We're inspecting the new security measures at the water sanitation plant. We need to make sure it's fully protected."

A pick-up truck behind them screeched its brakes and Keith hit the gas.

"Protected from what?" asked Sam.

Keith blew air out of his pursed lips, making a spitting sound. "Do you read the papers? What *doesn't* it need to be protected from, son?"

Keith began speaking slowly and quietly, as if patiently explaining something to a child. "Al Qaeda computers seized last year show terrorists are on the verge of turning the internet into a goddamn weapon. They could get remote control of our water systems, gas pipelines, electricity grid. Imagine 30,000 volts of electric power in the hands of al Qaeda. We're talking about a mass bloodshed event, sir." Keith paused for dramatic effect. "There is a credible threat they could poison our water."

Wendy turned around and, catching Sam's eyes, opened hers wide, a look of mock concern that told him, yes, Keith was serious.

Sam resolved not to ask any more questions. It was always hard for him to bite his tongue, but he had to be careful. He was in the presence of a true believer—one with a direct line to his boss. But maybe he also wanted to be quiet because of Wendy, because he wasn't sure if he could return her bright smile. He couldn't quite tell what she was thinking. Sam laced his fingers together and looked out the window.

As they headed west, downtown gave way to strip malls and then big box stores. They passed a Walmart that looked like a small village, an American flag—maybe fifteen, twenty feet long—snapping in the wind above a packed parking lot.

Then the stores gave way to harvested corn fields, the brown stubs of broken stalks protruding from the earth in neat rows, all leading to a single point on the horizon. After ten minutes of silent driving, Keith turned right, and after another five, they slowed to a stop in front of a twelve-foot-tall concrete wall, topped with barbed wire. The barrier wrapped around the perimeter of a facility that looked to be about the size of four football fields.

Above them, towering two, maybe three, stories over the entrance way, was a guard tower—a stalk of muted grey-green steel that gave way to a bulb on top. Inside, a man wearing all black. Sam squinted. Was that a rifle on his shoulder? An automatic weapon? Jesus, Keith wasn't the only person hunting for terrorists in the cornfields of Central Illinois.

Keith got out of the car, shut the door behind him, and immediately began huddling with three men who emerged from a gate in the wall. Sam and Wendy stood by the car, out of earshot of the others. "Water engineer, district manager, and head of security," said Wendy, pointing her finger three times.

"I don't understand why I'm here," said Sam.

"There's nothing to understand. They need to make it seem like the Commission is inspecting the plant's security progress. All you have to do is walk around and look at whatever they tell you to. And once in a while, nod your head like this." Wendy furrowed her brow and slowly nodded, as though Sam had said the most important thing in the world.

Sam meant to chuckle, but it came out a harsh bark—a laugh of disgust. Sam covered his mouth.

"I was supposed to be at a United Gas luncheon at the Hilton," said Wendy, with the slightest note of agreement. "Instead of white tablecloths and wine, I'm out here playing boy scout."

The tour started at the wall. "Twelve feet of concrete, topped by razor wire, this bad boy stretches all the way around the perimeter," said the head of security. "We cleared our blueprints with the FBI's new National Infrastructure Center."

Wait, he'd heard that before. The fifth-floor conference room, the man's hand on his back, the binder. Sam wrote in his notepad, "national infrastructure center?"

"They've identified the Smith, Illinois water plant as a potential al Qaeda soft target," the head of security added, his voice grave. "Do you know what a soft target is?" Before they could respond, he continued, "It's a target not normally secured that terrorists could attack to create panic and mayhem. It's vital to their broader War on Terror strateg—"

Wendy chimed in, "Out of curiosity, how many 'soft targets' are there?"

"Approximately 9,870 in the United States, ma'am. That's what makes this so important"

Sam jumped in, "If we're one in 10,000 wouldn't that make us fairly unimportant, by definition?"

"Did you see the President's speech last week?" the head of security said. "Everything has to be treated as a potential target and everyone a potential terrorist. We're at war, and securing the homeland is just as important as Afghanistan."

Keith stood with his hands on his hips, squinting as his head moved up and down, then side to side. "Not bad, boys. This has come a long way."

Wendy caught Sam's eye and he looked down at the wilted brown grass to stifle a smile. Sam fastened the top button of his coat as the wind made a rustling sound and a cloud cast a shadow over where they were standing.

"When Prairie Water says we need to protect consumers, we mean it," said the district manager. "One hundred percent of those rate increases went into building this wall."

Sam again scribbled, "rate increases?" This was the first Sam had heard of al Qaeda threats being used to justify spiking prices for consumers, no less for something like water, which people cannot live without. Sam wasn't sure what he believed anymore, but he knew that private utility companies were not to be trusted, that his job was to guard the public from their greed, even if all he was offering was a thin layer of protection—slightly greater odds people wouldn't be forced to choose between heat and paying rent. But water and sewer weren't even his purview. God, what was he doing here?

"Don't forget they also paid for that tower," the head of security said, pointing up then walking towards the base of the tower.

Sam, Keith, and Wendy followed him, but the rest stayed behind. When they reached the base of the guard tower, the head of security paused. "You go ahead. I'll wait down here." They nodded, and Keith led them up a narrow spiral staircase that winded towards an opening of light. Sam could hear Keith breathing heavily above him.

Stepping onto the lookout, Sam was met by a man with buzzed black hair and a permanent smirk. He had that type of complexion Sam noticed a lot in Central Illinois, that somehow glowed Irish bright red but was weathered at the same time. His black cargo pants were tucked into his combat boots, a black collared shirt bulging out of a bulletproof vest, sunglasses reflecting the fields in hues of purple and green. Sam saw his vest, just above his heart, was emblazoned with an image of an eagle, its talons reaching for the kill. The man's right hand was gently resting on the rifle that hung from his right shoulder, as if he were caressing a small animal.

He looks to be in his late twenties, thought Sam, a full decade older than the infantry soldiers they're shipping off to Afghanistan. They go in first because they're disposable—infantry aren't even required to have graduated high school.

Sam shuddered as he grabbed onto the rail and felt the wind toss his hair. Below him, surrounded by patches of dead grass, were six perfectly circular ground-level pools, each with a concrete circle at their center, like the pupil of an eye. At the top of each pool, railed walkways led from the perimeter to the center. Or at least he thought they were walkways. While Sam could imagine not much befalling these pools beyond the occasional leaf or bird dropping, he wondered how much the cost of running a bath had risen to pay for these heavily-armed grunts.

He looked over at Keith, who stood with his arms crossed talking to the man, a satisfied grin on his face, like he was reuniting with an old buddy, finally among friends. As Wendy walked towards Sam, the man followed her with his eyes, a faint look of hunger—or was it possessiveness? Is it possible, Sam hoped, this guy is threatened by me? Sam looked down at his scrawny arms then over at the man—broad-shouldered and wiry in his industrial GI Joe get-up. No, it's not possible.

Wendy joined Sam at the railing. "Quite a sight," he said.

"No better way to see Central Illinois than looking for terror plots." Wendy smiled as she made air quotes with her fingers. "Besides, the Hilton luncheon isn't nearly so exciting. They don't even have guns."

Sam looked over at her and laughed. The sun cast a golden light on her face. Shadows moved across her cheeks when she smiled.

"So what do you think so far?" Wendy looked out at the

horizon.

"Of the tower?"

"Springfield. It looks nice from up here."

Sam was confused. "But you can't even see it."

"Exactly."

Sam smiled. "You're not a fan either?"

"It's alright." Wendy turned to face him. "You moved here from Chicago?"

"How'd you know?"

"Aside from your extremely obvious eye rolling at our friend Keith back there, it's my job to look at personnel files. I know more than I probably should."

"I hope Keith doesn't think I dislike him. I actually find his earnestness refreshing."

"Rank-and-file usually are in my experience."

"So you read all the personnel files, huh?"

"Yeah."

"That doesn't seem fair. I don't know anything about you. You gotta tell me something."

"Well, okay, if I must. But you can't tell anyone."

"I swear."

"Pinky swear?"

"Double pinky swear."

"I'm part of an al Qaeda sleeper cell sent to infiltrate the Commerce Commission."

Sam let out a laugh that was quickly absorbed by the wind. She was hard to read and funny, two things Sam had a long history of falling for. He'd marched right into Springfield, jaded and uncertain about where he stood in the universe, determined to keep everyone at arm's length until he had some idea, but here he was, squirming in his shoes and flirting like a Middle Schooler. What the hell was going on?

He saw a sudden flash of black in his periphery and, when he looked over, realized the man in all black was staring at him, his eyes small. Sam looked away and let his gaze wander down to the base of the tower, which seemed taller from where they were—maybe three, four stories. He felt his knees go weak as he pictured himself toppling over.

"Hey I'm going to head down," he said to Wendy. "I think I've observed enough security measures."

Just as he let go of the railing he felt a hand on his shoulder. He remembered the man in the conference room, firmly handling him as he guided him out. Sam whipped around and reflexively put his hands out in front of him. He felt his left forearm knock against something long and metal. A rifle. "Jesus!" Sam shouted, the wind dampening his voice. "That can't be safe."

"Don't I know you?" The man was right in front of him, his voice insistent, aggressive even.

"No, I'm pretty sure you don't."

"Yeah, I swear I've seen you before."

"That's impossible. I just moved here."

"The gala last night. You were at the Healthy Futures Alliance. I saw you at the United Gas table."

Sam let out a wry smile. "Ah yes, you're right. That was me. You've got a good eye."

"An eagle eye," the man said, patting the logo on his vest, just above his heart. "I never forget a face. Ever."

The man's expression softened as Wendy approached. His eyes, so aggressive just a moment before, were pulled downward in a shy bow. "Ma'am, after you." He put out his hand for Wendy so that she could steady herself as she began her descent down the stairs. She took it with a smile that could have meant she was charmed by him, or polite, or something in between. "Name's Daryl," said the man. "Pleasure," she responded, her smile growing wider.

As she took Daryl's arm and went down the flight of stairs, Sam was embarrassed to find he was struck with a visceral sense of jealousy. They'd talked all of two minutes and certainly, if her goal was not to plunge to her death, someone who could pass as a stunt double for Jason Statham was a better bet than his wiry frame. He liked his chances better on the ground.

Chapter 6

The sun was still high as they drove the same route back, past the fields and department stores, back downtown. The metallic silver dome topping the state capitol, built in the architectural style of the French renaissance, clashed with the six-story parking garage to its left—a grid of grey concrete filled with shadows. A cylindrical hotel towered above it all, thirty stories higher than the next tallest building, like a guard tower looking over the city. As on the ride there, Sam had resolved to keep his thoughts to himself, but the strange tour of the plant's military-grade equipment played over and over in his mind, a record growing louder with each turn.

He blurted out, "Didn't that whole thing seem a bit militarized?"

"A bit militarized?" scoffed Keith. With his right hand he reached over Wendy's lap into the glove compartment, his left hand still on the wheel. He pulled out a newspaper and tossed it into the back seat with a violent flick, as if trying to scare away an animal. "Open that to the local section."

Sam pulled the paper taut and smoothed the page with his

hand. The issue was from August, when Sam had first driven to Springfield hoping his car wouldn't break down. He saw a photograph of a middle-aged woman standing in a field with a dire expression on her face, staring straight at the camera. Next to that, the headline, "Woman Spots Small Aircraft at Low Altitude Over Smith Water Facility, Calls 9-1-1."

Sam read the first paragraph. "They dispatched all those fire trucks and shut down the highway?" he said.

"Yup," said Keith. "And they never even found the unidentified aircraft."

"You can't honestly—"

"Hey," Wendy interrupted, "mind if we stop for coffee?" She shot a pleading expression at Sam as she pointed at a small storefront decorated with a blue neon sign shaped like a coffee cup with plumes of neon-yellow steam rising from it. Keith hit the brakes hard enough to make the tires squeal then pulled into the parking space out front. On the way in, Sam saw a red bike locked to the rack out front, a piece of paper taped to it. "Buy me," it said.

The second he opened the door, Sam inhaled a gust of coffee grounds mixed with dirty dishrags. The milk frother screamed and above that floated angry, wailing vocals punctuated with staccato guitar plucking. The barista was mouthing the words along while nodding her head, both hands on the pitcher in front of her. Her hair was purple and her right shoulder covered in star tattoos that grew smaller as they cascaded down to her elbow.

Keith walked up to the counter and put both of his hands on the wood surface, leaning forward, in what seemed an awkward attempt at striking a casual pose. As soon as he opened his mouth, his confidence and sureness melted away. "I'll have an, um, mocha latte—is that how you say it?" he said haltingly, making sure Wendy heard him. "Can't just get a simple cup of coffee anymore, everything's frapa that and vanilla this. Can't find coffee flavored coffee anymore."

The barista looked on, confused. "We have regular coffee, do you want that?"

Sam was about ninety percent sure Keith was rehashing a Denis Leary bit from some five years ago, which just made him feel bad for the guy. Keith stood up straight and stared intently at his shoes, as if he could make himself disappear, and sulked away from the counter. "Oh no, just something I had heard. Black coffee, please."

After everyone ordered, they sat down at a small circular table by a wall covered in flyers—kittens for sale, looking for a bassist, 'NIL8' show at the Atrium. When Sam's knee bumped against Wendy's, he pulled his leg away so hard he hit the table, spilling a splash from Keith's coffee. Keith jumped up and made his way to the napkins.

As soon as Keith turned his back to them, Wendy said in a harsh whisper, "Why are you arguing with him? You're not going to change his mind. What are you trying to get out of this?"

"I'm a sadist."

Wendy was unamused.

"I don't know." Sam switched to earnest mode for the first time and leaned in. "Everyone in this job, in this town, seems to have an incurable case of the 'aw shucks.' I take no pleasure in being a prick to this guy, but it's not like al Qaeda is going to storm Myrtle Beach tomorrow."

"That's not how these things work, not anymore."

"People keep saying this, yeah. So what, we're gonna treat the Sheboygan DMV like the Pentagon until... when exactly?"

"This isn't about political ideals, Sam, come on. Your problem's with hicks in general." Her voice was surprisingly savage. Sam recoiled a bit, realizing he'd taken their shared joke too far.

"I never—"

"They made me read your file, Sam, remember? I know about Seattle '99 and all the ski mask hijinks, so save the indignation. I'm not judging, hell, a couple drinks in and I'm partial. But in this business, it's important to tell the difference between actually having principles and the high one gets from feeling like they do."

A voice from afar interrupted the pause, "Wendy, latte, two percent, no foam."

"Let Keith do his job." She stood up. "It's silly 9/11 gave guys like him a plot, but maybe the people at Sheboygan DMV appreciate feeling like they matter now."

Before Sam could answer, Keith sat back down and began wiping the table. "Any plans for the holiday?" Keith asked, breaking the silence as he fidgeted with his wedding ring.

"I usually go back East for Thanksgiving, but I can't afford it this year," Sam said cheerily, taking Wendy's advice.

Wendy walked back with her latte, already buttoning up her coat with her left hand. "Hey, I'd better get back to the office."

"You guys go ahead," said Sam. "I'll meet you there." Wendy gave him a perplexed look but didn't argue. As soon as the two were out the door, Sam walked up to the counter. "I wanted to see about that bike."

The barista made a call on her cell phone and, ten minutes later, a guy with a dark beard and ponytail, wearing a baggy shirt with colorful bears dancing across a tie-dye swirl, showed up. The transaction was quick, and Sam tossed the bike-lock key in his palm as he walked out of the cafe. None of the tires were flat, and the seat seemed to reach right to his hips when he stood next to the bike. Things he should have checked before he bought it, it occurred to Sam, but he rarely did.

Sam's legs burned, and cold air tinged with diesel gas cycled through his lungs as he propelled himself past store fronts. A box truck flew past him so close he could feel its air suction pulling him in, and he pitched his weight to the right to steady himself. He tried to clear his head, but the events of the day seemed to morph and bend like putty—the tower, the armed guards, the barbed wire, Wendy's cutting humor and brittle anger.

Sam saw a green sign with white lettering that said, "OFF-TRACK BETTING." He pulled the breaks with his hands and looked in, but the storefront was dark, and he couldn't tell if it was open. Sam had gone once in Chicago—he'd liked how it felt like an underworld in broad daylight, people shouting and muttering in front of screens, the constant threat of ruin in the air. But he also liked the rush of winning—the rare feeling when he jumped and actually landed.

A horn went off and then someone was screaming at him. "Get out of the road, faggot!" the last word fading away as the car drove out of earshot. Sam jumped off his bike and walked it on the sidewalk the half block to his office. I'll let that guy win this time, he thought to himself, his heart pounding.

He couldn't find a bike rack, so he pulled it up the steps and onto the elevator. When Dee Dee saw him rolling his bike onto the fourth floor, she turned her eyebrows into little arches high on her forehead and just left them there—a look of bored shock—

but Sam rolled past, pretending not to notice.

Sam stopped in the hallway, holding his bike by the handles. Julie, John, and Jack were clustered in front of his office door, obstructing his path with a heated debate about high school football.

"I know for a fact his aunt doesn't live in Chatham," said Julie.

"Oh, I don't know, Chatham's different now," said Jack. "Ever since they built those housing projects in Trevi Springs."

"But his aunt goes to Missionary Baptist," said Julie. "Why would she drive from Chatham to the East Side every Sunday?"

"Well, you drive from Johnstown to Springfield every day."

"I have no choice. Besides, I go to church in Johnstown."

"All I know," John cut in, "is that the Chatham Hawks would never be in the playoffs right now without his natural talent."

Sam took a step towards his office, rolling his bike along with him. The Triple J's looked at him at the same time.

"What are you doing with that?" asked Jack with a sardonic smile. "Are you in grade school?"

Sam heard his phone ring in his office. "Excuse me, I have to get that," he said, rolling his bike through their huddle. Jack pressed himself up against the wall in an exaggerated motion, as though Sam were wildly wielding a dangerous instrument.

"Greg," Sam said when he answered the phone. "You're a lifesaver."

As soon as he hung up, Sam heard tapping on his door.

Dee Dee walked in carrying a large box. When she dropped it on Sam's desk, he saw it was full of papers.

"Charlie wants you to testify on the United Gas rate case. Here's the company's filing. This sheet tells you when testimony is due. Let Charlie know if you have any questions."

"Wait, what? Why me? Isn't this a giant company? I just started."

"They're all giant companies, hon." Dee Dee shot him a smile. "They must think you're special."

Sam couldn't tell if she was being sarcastic. "Is this normal? Those other guys you mentioned, the other Junior Analysts under Charlie, did they also get United this early?"

"Sweetie, 'Junior Analyst for Charlie' *is* United. United's his baby, you're the midwife."

"Well, uh, can I talk to Charlie?"

"He's still at the Hilton luncheon with these guys." Dee Dee patted the box.

"Do you know when he'll be back?"

Dee looked at Sam and smiled. "What do you think?" She was already out the door.

Sam sat looking at the box, rubbing his thumb against his right forefinger. He remembered his first day at TGI Friday's on the cook line, the sweltering steam and grease that jumped up from the stove, biting him. Somehow he got through it, forced his body to chop, flip, fry, remember orders. But he also had help. "Why are you so fucking slow, man," Jorge would always say. "Here, let me do it."

Sam walked down to Greg's office and stood in the doorway. "Got my first case."

"Let me guess—a delivery from Dee Dee."

"Yeah. I have no idea what I'm doing. I'm in the deep end now."

"Been there. Want some help? I can stay late tonight if you want."

The room was silent, and Greg looked at Sam with an expectant expression. He felt his stomach tighten—that familiar feeling of exhilaration and dread, as though the decision had already been made, and he just had to watch himself do it. "Let's get out of the office," said Sam. "I have a crazy idea."

Chapter 7

The room buzzed with voices murmuring and shouting, but the cacophony wasn't jovial. The woman at the front desk looked at Sam's box of folders labeled "United," then at him, and shrugged her shoulders. "Two dollars to get in. Paying for both of you?"

Sam fumbled through the wad of $200 he'd withdrawn on the way over. He knew taking out a fifth of his life's savings was unwise, but the decision was made the moment Greg uttered a hesitant "yes" to Sam's offer: A $15 bet of his choosing for every fifteen minutes they spent on the testimony together. "You don't have to pay me to help you with this," Greg had said. "I'll do it either way." But Sam had persisted. "It'll be fun. I need a little adventure." Sam normally found it painful to pay more than $20 for a pair of pants, but once in a while, he liked to feel what it was like to wager almost everything.

The packed crowd did not make way—dozens stood fixated in front of the six television screens on the right wall, each showing grainy images of different horse races. "Way to go, chalky Charlie!" shouted a woman in her sixties in a long-sleeved leopard-print dress, pumping her fists in the air. A man next to her in a beige trench coat and green beanie was growling to himself, arms crossed in front of him. The smell of french-fry grease and body odor reminded Sam of the dingy bars in the cities he'd moved through—worlds far away from Springfield.

They sat down at two empty chairs across from each other at a long wooden table, and Sam put the box between them.

"Hey, can I ask you something?"

Greg nodded his head forward and held it there, studying Sam's face.

"What's the deal with Wendy? Do you know her?"

Greg smiled, but he didn't look pleased. "I've never gotten to know her, but she seems very smart. How do I put this? She's close with Charlie."

"You mean in a relationship or something?"

"No, I'm not saying that. But they're allies. On the same team."

"She didn't seem particularly on-program when I talked to her."

"What did she say?"

"Oh nothing, she just seemed like, you know, a real person."

"Well then, what do I know?"

Greg pulled open his wallet but Sam put out his hand. "Tonight's on me." He noticed one half of a picture protruding out. "Who's that?"

Greg peeled it out, a smiling woman whose face was framed by blonde feathers of hair and a crown of tall, sprayed bangs.

"My wife—she's five months pregnant. I recommend dating civilians, if you can get any of them to come near you."

"Oh wow, congratulations, man. Let me buy you a beer."

A woman with fire truck red hair who walked with a limp handed Sam two Miller Lites. When he got back to the table, Greg was squinting at a page in front of him. "What a blowhard," he said when Sam sat down.

Sam took the paper out of Greg's hands. "Oh—Thomas French? I met him the other night. He was handing some kid a giant check."

"Read that and you'll see what he was doing with the other hand." Greg tossed him five more pages.

Sam took a slug of his beer and tried to focus his eyes in the dim light, covering his ears with his hands. As the noise muted into a dull buzz, he began to absorb the words. He learned Mr. French cared deeply about customers and, yes, they had just been hit with two consecutive rate increases. The last thing he wanted to do, allegedly, was to raise their rates again, but United supposedly had no choice. Mr. French claimed the company faced spiraling costs and stagnating revenues and it had done everything and beyond to address the situation but was forced to ask for one more increase.

Sam took a few more gulps of his beer. Mr. French said the Company had anguished for many days over this matter. When his accountants had insisted that United seek a 15 percent increase, he'd put his foot down. "That would just be unfair to the poor ratepayers." So Mr. French pared his request down to a barebones 11.5 percent per year, supposedly the absolute minimum needed to cover costs and generate a reasonable return for United's long-suffering shareholders.

After a few minutes, Sam asked, "Is he threatening us?"

"What do you mean?" Greg had a sardonic expression on his face.

"He says the company needs more money now in order to lower rates in the future. And if they don't get what they want, they'll be forced to come back far sooner—and ask for much, much more."

Greg let out a soft chuckle. "United got a 12 percent rate increase eleven months ago and a 9 percent twelve months before that," he said. "They're not so much threats as demands."

"Well, then, what are we doing here?"

"Winning some money. You owe me. It's been fifteen minutes." Sam chuckled as Greg pulled a beaten racing book closer to him. "The whole pseudoscience with the books and the who did what in what weather, it's maddening," Greg said, setting down the book labeled 11/01/02.

"Yeah?"

"Me? I always play the Greg Caldwell system, it's foolproof. You see, the last four digits of my social—"

"How's that?"

"8274. Whatever race is 8 minutes to post, then 2, 7, 4 to win, place, and show. Swear to god I've won hundreds of dollars on this system. It's uncanny. I don't need a lucky number, I *am* the lucky number."

"You're so full of shit," Sam said with a half-curious laugh. He was starting to feel the beers.

"I am, but not on this. I swear by it."

Sam scanned the room until he saw a race that was eight minutes until post.

"Saratoga Downs?" he said, gesturing towards a TV behind Greg.

Greg said, "If it's MTP 8 minutes, then yes, let's do it."

The camera followed a brown horse carrying a small jockey on his back over a track so wet it reflected the gray sky. It was number two, the favored winner. Sam was struck by how unceremonious the scene looked, the drab clothes and blank expressions, like he was watching someone work a job they hated. "Sloppy fucking track," said the man at the end of the table.

"I'm putting all mine on big number six," Sam said to Greg.

"You do know he's 40 to 1."

Sam shot back, "You know you bet a government issued number, right?"

"Touché."

"Track's wet," said Sam. "You never know what can happen. Besides, horse's name is Thanatos' Drive and I'm a sucker for irony."

Sam came back with their tickets just as the horses took off. Number two pulled in front, the jockey's head pitched forward, hips in the air, as advertisements scrolled across the bottom of the screen. Sam couldn't see number six until the horse pulled just behind number two. Eight was behind both of them.

A crowd had gathered, and murmurs mixed with shouts.

Suddenly number two lurched to the right, and his front legs collapsed. The jockey flew off of him and rolled in the mud before waving his hands in the air. Number eight veered out of the way, and six whizzed by and passed through the finish line. Seven was just behind and inched over the finish line ahead of eight. The camera shot to the jockey, standing next to horse two, still on its side in the same place where he fell.

The sudden violence had a disquieting effect on Sam, though he was pleased to have won—it was real money for him. He looked over at Greg, casually sipping his beer, and decided not to say anything. The whole enterprise was seedy, and it was usually agreed upon in these manly contexts to not give in to sentiment.

"Rough one for that guy, huh?" Sam glibly let out.

"No shit." Greg quickly shifted gears. "You're a rich man, next round's on you."

When Sam came back from the bar with two more Miller Lites, Greg was looking over another stack. "Meet Albert Klough," Greg said, handing him a large file.

Sam looked over the file. The next witness had the mission of discussing some of the pesky costs the company could not control. Mr. Klough talked about the Company's charitable contributions to the Healthy Futures Alliance—rising because of the pain and difficulty felt by so many of their customers.

"Why were these contributions discussed in a rate case?" Sam noticed his speech slurring and sat up straighter.

"The company collects those charitable donations from ratepayers."

"So United is parading around as if it cares about the poor and downtrodden while really taking the money from ratepayers, many of whom are poor and downtrodden themselves? That One Springfield meeting I went to—"

"I know."

Sam looked down and the words were blurring together, anger warming into a slow burn. "So, ratepayers foot the bill so United can afford to hire the lawyers and consultants who best help them raise rates as much as possible?"

"Wait until you get to the part where he says the company needs more money so that it can protect the public against terrorist threats."

"You can't be serious."

"Where do you think Prairie Water got the money for the guard tower?"

"Do they ever talk about, you know, run-of-the-mill boring stuff, like maintaining gas line infrastructure? Or is it all playing mall cop against some terrorist threat?"

"Honestly, since September 11, it's more of the latter."

Sam threw the pages down on the table and leaned towards Greg. "I hate to say it, but the stereotypes about lazy state workers seem to be ringing true. Charlie can't stop golfing and the Triple J's can't stop talking about high school football long enough to regulate these companies at all."

"No, that's bullshit," said Greg. "This has nothing to do with being lazy. I worked at a grocery store for ten years before I got this job. But the more I do think about our job, the more I think libertarians may be right."

"How so?"

"The way regulators are completely beholden to a handful of big companies. It makes me think regulation is really just a way for big firms to keep out the little guy."

"This comes up a lot in Marxist circles."

"Not a sentence you hear every day in Springfield."

"Look, United is a natural monopoly—it's not like you're going to have multiple gas lines going into people's houses." Greg was nodding his head impatiently, as if to say, 'Yes, I know this already,' but Sam plowed ahead. "So those executives figured out they'd rather be regulated than hand their goods over to public control, although public control makes the most sense, even according to the logic of capitalism, since there's no competition. Hell, executives prefer having the Commerce Commission, so long as the utility companies are able to hire all these assholes who are pros at gaming the system and finding ways around regulation. So now utilities are making more in profits than the free market would ever give them. And with all these regulators, it looks like the oversight system is robust."

Sam took a big gulp of his beer. "But the solution isn't to just throw your hands up and not regulate, it's to chip away the power of the private utility sector, use every tool you have to stick up for the little guy. Of course, it would be much better to have publicly-owned and run utilities, so that the little guy isn't just 'protected'—but calling the shots."

"Like Smith City Lights and Power?" said Greg, before taking a slug of his beer. "That's your ideal model? They're publicly owned."

"They're hardly a model of democratic public ownership," said Sam. "The people who run that town are so conservative they have about the most regressive rate structure you could

78

imagine. And they're completely in the pocket of coal. If we put utilities under real public control, that would just be the first step. We'd have to convince the city to go renewable and finally start to tackle the issue of global warming…" Sam's voice trailed off.

Greg's face crumpled into a sneer. "Man, you are on another planet. Try convincing Charlie that global warming is real, or that our job is to protect the little guy, let alone try convincing any powerful person in this city that we should take over United Gas." His laughter came out in a choke. "They'd want to know if you'd like gulags with your Soviet-style utility."

"There's a large gap between public control of utilities and gulags."

"Not to the Illinois business community there isn't."

Greg's expression grew serious as he leaned towards Sam. "You want to know why the 'lazy state worker' barb is a fallacy? When you know your work doesn't matter, that the people at the top don't want you to do your job, and will devote considerable resources to stop you from doing it well, most people stop trying. And a small, doomed minority become defiant."

"Which are you?"

"I keep my feelings inside. And if you're smart, you will too."

Sam rubbed the burn on his forefinger with his thumb and looked at Greg, whose eyes seemed moist, face puffy from beer and bar nuts. "I don't think you have to worry about me," Sam said. "If you'd asked me a few years ago, that'd be a different story." Sam paused. "What about the true believers? Keith, that Captain America guy from inspections?"

Greg laughed. "Yeah, he's a trip."

"I went with him to inspect the water sanitation plant's security system, and I swear he wanted to arm the guards with manpads."

"People like him do well here."

"And what about people who aren't like him?"

Greg shifted his chair. "There was this one inspector, middle-aged, nice, kind of nerdy. He'd only been working here a few months before he just kind of vanished. All of a sudden his name placard was down from his door, and security escorted him out of the building. Can you imagine that? I don't think I've ever seen the security guard get up from his chair before or since."

"What did he do?"

"I never found out, but there was this sense that it was something horrible. People wouldn't even speak his name, like he was Voldemort."

"He was shunned?"

"Well, that's assuming he wanted to talk to any of us."

Sam smiled. "And you haven't heard anything from him in all these years?"

"Actually, it was just six months ago."

"Oh." Sam felt his stomach go weak. "What about the last guy who had the United case? Did he also disappear?"

"Oh, Bill? He was out of here in, like, six months, but that was different. He was happy as a clam. Got some other position. I think he still goes golfing with Charlie."

"Huh. Why is there so much turnover?"

"I don't know. But I'm telling you, lay low."

"Listen," Sam said, "I really appreciate you showing me the ropes. Your turn." He held up his wad of cash, thicker than when they had walked in, and pointed to a race that was nine minutes out.

As Sam walked up to the counter, he felt his focus go in and out, as though rotating the lens on a camera. He wove through a dozen people clustered around a screen mounted on the other wall, their movements frantic, one man in the back leaning into his cane and shouting, "No! No!"

"Forty on number one," Sam told the woman at the counter. "And this is for my friend," said Sam, giving Greg's bet.

It was another muddy track, this time with jockeys pulled behind in wagons, their small bodies strange appendages to the lean, muscular horses.

"What did you decide?" asked Greg.

"Not telling."

"Wagering your bets on bloodshed again?"

This time, the race went smoothly. No horses crumpled like felled trees, no jockeys flew through the air. Number eight sailed through the finish line in first place, as expected, and number one came in dead last, as expected.

Greg's face was frozen in a wide grin. His silly social security number system had paid off, Sam thought. He handed Greg his ticket and felt bile start to climb his throat. Yearning for bed, he wondered if Gertrude would be up and try to bother him on his way into the apartment.

When Greg came back with his money, Sam was packing up the box.

"I'm cutting myself off for the night."

"But we were just getting started, " Greg said, high with victory.

"I really appreciate your help, man. It was really nice of you."

"My pleasure."

They shook hands and Sam zipped up his coat. "Maybe you're right that I should lay low."

"Somehow, I doubt you will."

Chapter 8

Sam's sweat evaporated in shivers as he zigzagged his way home, holding the box in his right hand and pulling the bike with his left over cracked sidewalks threaded with brown grass. Two blocks from the OTB, he leaned too hard into his bike, and despite his attempt to swing his weight in the other direction, fell onto its hard frame, landing flat on his side. Papers strewn around him, Sam imagined what his brother would say—"You can't hold your liquor at all," a smug smile plastered to his face. Sam sat up and started slowly collecting the pages, legs sprawled out in front of him in a v-shape.

He heard a voice behind him. "Sam, is that you?"

Wendy. She wore a green peacoat over a tight black dress. A man stood behind her. Sam couldn't bring himself to look at the man's face, but he made out broad shoulders and an expensive-looking suit jacket.

"Are you okay?" The concern in her eyes, outlined in charcoal and shadow, was touching. But then Sam glimpsed the man behind her in his periphery—a blank space, a person-shaped cutout. Sam felt the bile begin to climb back up.

"Just being my usual, graceful self." Sam reached for the hand Wendy had extended to him, gripping it tight as she tugged him to his feet. "And you?"

"More graceful than you!" Wendy let out a sharp laugh.

"No, I mean, how's your night going?" Sam smiled shyly.

"We were just coming from dinner." Wendy pointed with her thumb towards the man standing behind her. Sam wondered if she was going to introduce him, but she didn't. Instead she stood with her thumb extended for a moment before slowly lowering her hand to her side.

Sam looked at the man's face—he was just as handsome as feared, but in the starting quarterback way Sam would never be: square jaw, thick neck, cheeks doused in freckles that somehow also looked manly.

Sam had extended his arm slightly in front of him, anticipating a shake, but slipped it into his pocket instead. He noticed Wendy studying him intently. Is she worried about what I think, he wondered, does she want me to be jealous? When he caught her eye she looked at the ground, then squatted low, balancing on her heels as she started collecting papers. Sam crouched down and did the same, while Wendy's presumptive date remained upright.

Wendy held up a piece of paper. "Albert Klough, eh? That man's about as thrilling as a root canal."

Sam laughed. "They have me on the new United case."

"I know."

"How?"

"It's a small office."

"He's pretty corrupt, Klough," Sam lamented. "A week on the job and it seems they're all pretty corrupt, backslapping at dinners with the people we're supposed to be regulating, talking in code."

"Yeah well, it's not a wholly original observation."

"Hey, Wendy, we should go," the man called out. Does this guy always sound like a busy manager barking orders at an intern? Sam wondered.

Still crouching, Wendy said, "I guess we have to go. Don't work too hard."

"Isn't that the Commerce Commission's mantra?"

"Well, some of us normal people try."

"Look, I think we got off on the wrong foot. My barely concealed contempt for, you know," Sam looked around him. "This situation—"

"You're gonna say it's masking a hidden vulnerability and insecurity, and that I should see you as a prick with a heart of gold, and understand that underneath the pot shots is a jaded ex-radical simply looking for a home."

"Actually, I was just gonna say it's because all our coworkers are racist layabouts, but yeah, your version sounds good too."

"Your resentment is 100 percent authentic and that's fine, whatever. Your problem, as I see it, having known you for all of ten hours, is that it's completely misplaced."

"Yeah?"

The man called out again, "Wendy come on, they're not gon-na hold our table forever!"

"Children get mad at situations, Sam. Angsty teenagers lash out at 'shitty towns' and 'lame jobs.'" She shoved the box in his arms. "Adults target the source of their anger and do something about it. You're a regulator, you don't like these people, regu-late." Wendy turned around and called after the man. "Coming!"

Sam stood there alone, United box in hand. He couldn't help but smile. "Okay, she's good," he whispered to no one.

On the walk home, his mind was a whirring engine. Maybe Wendy was right—he was filled with venom, constantly flaunting his ability to diagnose the world's ills. But what was underneath, what did his core consist of? It had been two years since he'd done any real organizing—actually fought for something, really committed. He was nothing, a leaf shaken loose from a tree, all alone, blowing from one city to the next. Sam's slow footsteps echoed in the quiet, the moon casting pale shadows over yards and rooftops. He felt as though he were being pulled by a current.

Gertrude intercepted him in the stairway, her sharp voice trig-gering his adrenaline. "What are you doing? You smell like beer. Vhy are you out so late?"

"Gertrude, I'm sorry, I don't have time for this right now."

"Hold on. I have key for you." Gertrude pulled out a key from her pocket and held it towards Sam. "I get keychain from hardware store so you don't lose."

Sam looked at the circular keychain, dangling from her pinched fingers. It read, "Home of Lincoln" in black lettering, outlined in green. Behind those words, a silhouette of the young Lincoln, without his tall hat.

Something about the sight of that keychain made Sam pause. It seemed so permanent, so official—he now lived in Springfield, the "Home of Lincoln." But now that he was holding a ticket to the comfortable, secure life he had sought through endless job applications, he wanted to tear it up—or maybe just give it to someone else for safekeeping, at least until he'd decided exactly what he was willing to give of himself for the comfort of knowing how he was going to pay rent and buy groceries for the next year, five years, ten? Sam pushed the keychain away with his palm. "You know what, I'll just leave it unlocked for now. I don't have anything to steal anyway."

Sam slammed the apartment door behind him. He walked over to his record player and put on a record his mother loved, La Traviata, and a man's voice began soaring over the staccato pulsing of a symphony. Sam was no expert in opera but he liked its intensity—its conviction that the human condition is profound and worthy of deep feeling.

Sam sat down in front of his desktop computer, heard the beeping and static as the dial-up connected to the internet. His hands were shaking, face covered in a film of fresh sweat. I do believe in something, he thought, remembering the exhaustion of a day on the picket line for his university's sanitation workers. He had spent money he didn't have to buy donuts, stayed out every day until sunset, remained at the end to pack up picket signs. Because being a socialist means you always stay to help, and you do it over and over again, without ever knowing if you'll win.

Sam's thoughts wandered back to Wendy, her cheeks brushed pink and eyes turning from warm to fiery. He thought of the look on Mrs. Belinda's face when Sam said he had to leave, like a light had been turned off, the shutters pulled closed. He thought of the man from inspections who just vanished one day—he hadn't even caught his name. Sam wrote the data requests without pausing, first to Thomas French, then to Albert Klough. An

87

aria climbed in the background—a woman's voice, high and trembling. He had always been a fast typer, and it poured out of him, his fingers following the rhythm of the music. No, you can't just raise the rates anytime you wish, citing specious claims about rising costs and terrorism and modernizing the grid. No, you can't force old women to huddle by their stoves, faces inches from red-hot burners. I can see exactly how vicious you are, Sam thought to himself, and it's my job to protect the public against you.

He re-read what he wrote only once, to comb the email for correct grammar and spelling, and entered the addresses of United's attorney, Albert Klough, Thomas French, and Charlie. Sam pressed send before he could stop himself. And then there was just the sound of the music—teeming harmonies punctuated with the woman's voice, harsh and rich, a beautiful scream. Sam put his arms around his stomach and bent at the middle, his face pressed to his knees as vertigo overtook him. This, Sam thought to himself, this is who I am.

Chapter 9

Sam waved at the security guard as he walked into the office the next morning, a calm smile on his face, and got onto the elevator, trying to ignore the queasy feeling in his stomach. He said hello to Dee Dee at her desk, but she just stared at him, jaw agape, as she slowly lowered her phone. Sam could feel her watching him as he **walked** toward his office. He straightened his posture and made his steps more deliberate. Act like you're sure of yourself, he thought, like you've done nothing wrong.

Really, I haven't, Sam assured himself. It was his job to send queries in response to the company's testimony, and that's what he had done. Sure, he sent it at one o'clock in the morning, his questions probably far more probing than the norm. But he hadn't thrown a grenade at anything—not yet.

When Sam turned down the hallway to his office, he saw Angelo pushing that same trash can.

"Rough night?" said Angelo.

"I look that bad?"

"Yep." Angelo smiled. "And whatever you did, people are

not happy."

"Did you get a read on Charlie yet?"

"Well, his door has been closed all morning, but I could make out muffled yelling over the phone."

"That's not good."

"Didn't sound like a chat with his dear mother, no." Angelo looked quizzical. "What'd you do?"

"My job. Which apparently is a major offense around here."

Angelo gave a weary chuckle. "Good luck with it, man." He pushed past Sam, who swung open the door to his office.

Sam barely stopped himself from shouting when he saw a man sitting in the chair across from his desk, in a relaxed pose, legs crossed loosely at the knees.

"Sorry, I—"

The man smiled at Sam, who stood frozen in the doorway. It was Phil.

"Oh, hi, I'm surprised to see you." As Sam said this, he realized that, somehow, he wasn't.

"Have a seat." Phil gestured towards Sam's chair.

"Uh, thanks for inviting me to take a seat in my own office."

"Sure, sure." Phil had the calm smile of a yoga instructor, and Sam sheepishly took a seat.

"Listen." Phil paused, sitting upright in Sam's chair, hands folded in his lap. "You have managed to get my supervisors a bit excited."

"How do you mean?"

"Look, you have opinions about United. Let me tell you: I do too. I get it. I don't want to put you in a box, man. I just want to make sure we're going about these things in a manner that's non-confrontational. That's the best way to really express the mutual interests of us and the people, don't you think?"

"Those data requests fall within the purview of my job."

"Of course they do. But this isn't about being on opposing sides. All that talk, all that thinking, is a dead end. It's not healthy. We should be focusing on the 'cans,' not the 'can'ts,' saying more yesses and fewer nos."

Phil lowered his voice and pressed the palms of his hands together, as if in prayer. "The Commerce Commission typically has a synergistic relationship with United, because our great partnership allows us to accomplish great things. Your information requests were, how shall I put this, overly burdensome. You and I both know your testimony is due in only three weeks, and we're concerned for you."

Sam cocked a brow. "Concerned?"

Phil smiled. "Of course. All this extra information could… unnecessarily complicate the process."

"I don't need you to tell me my timeline, Phil."

Phil smiled warmly, as though they were arguing over an inside joke. "Come on, Sam. You asked us to show every item we would purchase to improve our anti-terror efforts, as well as proof of what the costs would be. You wanted us to prove we had accepted three bids from three different companies on each item. Do you have any idea what kind of work that takes?"

"It's standard."

"Look man, these aren't standard times. There's a lot of hate out there." Phil gazed out of the window, a troubled expression on his face, as if he were on a movie set. Sam had to stop himself from laughing.

Phil looked back at Sam. "And you wanted a list of every charitable donation, the reasoning and outcome for each dollar given?"

"I know what I wrote, Phil."

"It's like United is being punished for giving back to the community. Look, this relationship doesn't work without trust. I put in a good word for you when you applied because I trust you, Sam. And I'm hoping you can repay me with your trust."

At summit protests, Phil had emphasized the importance of revolutionary discipline—that everyone stick unwaveringly to a group decision. Sam wondered if Phil was being disciplined now.

"Well, presumably when you recommended me you knew what kind of person I am."

"I knew that you were having a rough time, that you needed a friend." Phil let out a magnanimous chuckle. "Let's not kid ourselves, man. We're not who we were then. I'm changing the system from the inside now. So are you."

"How is that?"

"Everything starts with culture. It's how you treat each oth-er." Fingers upwards, Phil moved his hands in a circle as he said this. "All I'm asking for is respect and trust."

"Look, Phil, I'm trying to do due diligence. I'm not trying to foment insurrection. I'm just asking questions that fall within the purview of the duties I'm required to perform. The question of how we treat each other involves a whole lot more people than just you and me sitting in this room. I'm accountable to millions of ratepayers."

"I'm accountable to them too—and a company of 6,000 employees. I take my responsibilities very seriously." Phil placed a hand to his heart.

Suddenly the room was a whir of motion. Charlie had barged in, pushing the half-open door so hard it banged against the wall. He walked over to Phil, bent over and whispered something in his ear. Phil squinted and rapidly nodded his head.

When he looked up, Charlie turned to Sam. "I don't know what the hell got into you last night, but today's your lucky day. I was gonna staple your ass to the wall, but now I have to go deal with something more urgent."

"What ha—"

Before Sam could finish the question, the two men were out the door.

***

*

Sam walked into the hallway. It was empty—not totally unheard of for this early hour. He headed towards Dee Dee's desk, but she wasn't there, her cell phone resting on her empty chair. He heard the low murmur of voices start and then stop all at once, like a CD turning on and off. It sounded like it was coming from the break room, a place he usually avoided, turned off by the odor of sour coffee and the likelihood of finding one of the triple J's by the water cooler.

Sam paused at the doorway. The triple J's were sitting on plastic folding chairs facing the television mounted to the far wall, their backs to Sam. Greg and Dee Dee were just in front of him—from behind it looked like their arms were crossed. And Wendy, leaning against the wall on the right, back in her office clothes, this time beige. She was straining towards the television, her neck stretched forward.

In the room, a smattering of voices. "I told you," said Jack.

"We haven't seen any evidence," Greg replied.

Dee Dee walked over to Julie and whispered in her ear.

Sam took a step into the breakroom. "What's going on?"

Everyone went silent at once, as though a speaker had been ripped out of the wall. The entire room turned around to look at him. Wendy found Sam's eyes with hers, a stricken expression on her face, her forehead wrinkled into rivulets, mouth pursed into a dot. It seemed like she was trying to warn him about something, or maybe signal that she was sorry for last night, Sam hoped.

Jack broke the silence and looked at Sam. "We have real enemies out there, Sam. And I gotta tell ya, I don't think United is one of them."

Sam frantically searched the room looking for a friend, some-one to shield him from whatever innuendo was being hurled at him. He didn't dare look back in Wendy's direction. Something in her expression had jarred him.

When he met Greg's eyes, Greg cleared his throat. His voice was thin. He looked away from Sam, back at the rest of the room. "Look, we don't even know what we're dealing with here."

"Quiet," said Dee Dee. "The governor's speaking."

Sam stood next to Greg and peered at the television. He saw a tall man in a yellow tie lean into six microphones, a stocky police officer standing behind him to his left, his jaw angled upwards. Police lights reflected off of the white van behind them. A "breaking news" banner scrolled across the bottom of the screen.

"Today's incident has been deeply upsetting for the people of Springfield," said the governor. "We are saddened to learn of the death of Raphael Sanchez, the only person in Springfield High School at the time of the explosion."

"Oh god," Wendy muttered under her breath. Sam wanted to put his hand on her shoulder.

"Police and first responders continue to investigate the scene," the governor continued. "State and federal partners are joining us in our efforts. This is a fluid situation, and we will continue to inform the public as we obtain more information about the cause of this morning's events."

The governor's eyes darted to each of the six or seven cameras in front of him. "Rest assured, we are doing everything possible to secure the safety of the Springfield community."

Sam leaned towards Greg. "An explosion?" he whispered.

"Gas line. Seven in the morning. Thankfully no kids were at school yet."

"United?"

"Yup."

"Jesus. How long—"

"The news just broke."

Sam suddenly became aware of the throbbing in his temples, growing heavier in the unnatural shine of the fluorescent light. During the few hours of sleep he got between pressing send and walking up the stairs to the Commission, the company he was tasked with regulating had suffered an explosion. Suffered—or perpetrated? The most likely explanation was bad pipes, Sam thought, feeling a shudder move down his spine.

The police chief was talking now, his jaw still cocked upwards, as if held in place by a marionette string. "United Gas is fully cooperating with the investigation, and we have not ruled out an act of terrorism. We've raised the threat level for Central Illinois and are in discussions with the Office of Homeland Security and Attorney General Ashcroft to, perhaps, do the same nationally. All Springfield-area schools are closed until further notice."

"Why would he say that word?" Sam whispered to Greg.

Just then, out of the corner of his eye, Sam saw Wendy whip around towards the doorway. Charlie was in the hallway, standing next to a tall, thin man in a suit. He looked familiar, Sam thought, suddenly remembering the conference room he wandered into, the man who'd whisked him out, carrying a binder that said "InfraGard." It was him.

Wendy walked towards the door. But when she passed by Sam, she caught his eye. There was something searching in her expression, but Sam couldn't read it. He wanted to follow after her, ask what she was trying to say, or maybe just talk—about anything. Wendy walked through the doorway and into the hall.

Sam watched as the three walked away, their strides picking up pace.

***

Sam was sitting in his office with his door shut when he heard a knock. It was Greg, holding a small, toy basketball hoop in one hand and double-sided tape in the other. "I'm officially gifting this to you," he said as he affixed the hoop to Sam's wall. "You need it more than me."

"How so?"

"I've never been good at taking deep breaths. When I need to cool down, I wad up a piece of paper like this." Greg tore a piece of paper from a notebook on Sam's desk and handed it to him. Sam tossed it at the basket, missing the net completely.

"I'm horrible."

"The worse you are the better. Gives you more time to think."

Sam wadded up a piece of paper and with a flick of his right hand swished it through the basket. Greg sat in the chair across from Sam's desk, watching him.

"What were you thinking last night?"

"You're right, I never shoulda put fifty bucks on that quinella box at Saratoga."

"I'm being serious."

"It's hard to explain. Those people—"

"United?"

"You can't trust them. They're vultures." Sam ripped out another piece of paper and threw it hard, hand reaching back over his shoulder, like a baseball pitcher. The wad bounced off the wall and went through the net.

"No shit. That's exactly why you have to be careful."

"I sure have good timing, don't I? Everyone probably thinks I placed the bomb."

"That hasn't been ruled out yet."

Sam laughed. "You and I both know the likeliest explanation." He tore another page out and slowly folded it into a small cube. "Funny, I didn't see anything in that testimony about upgrading their pipes."

As Sam ripped out another piece of paper, Greg said, "I need you to listen to what I'm saying."

"I am listening. You're the one who brought this in here."

Greg slowly exhaled. "I don't know what you're trying to do. But do it deliberately. Think." Greg tapped his own skull with his forefinger then walked out of Sam's office, shutting the door behind him.

Sam picked up the papers from the floor, put them in the trash, then turned on his computer—something he hadn't yet had a chance to do that day. He'd expected multiple replies to his query, but he saw none. There was, however, a message from an unknown email address.

"Hi, this is Allison, the journalist you met at the One Springfield meeting. I was able to look you up on the Commerce Commission's website. I'm sure you heard about the horrible explosion this morning at Springfield High School. I was wondering if you'd be willing to answer a few questions about United—I know you're on the case."

Jesus, she really is the journalist Charlie warned us about, Sam thought. I'd never have pegged her for that.

"For your own protection," she continued, "I recommend you email me back from your personal account. As I'm sure you know, this address can be monitored by your employer, and subjected to FOIA requests. As I said before, we can speak completely off the record, or anonymously—it's up to you."

Sam remembered the warning from Greg, and the threat from Phil. Had that been that earlier today? It felt like last week. "Don't do anything yet," Sam said out-loud to himself. "Have a plan first."

Sam pulled out a piece of paper and wrote down Allison's email address, then moved the mouse to delete her message. As he put the piece of paper with the email address into his pocket, his hands were shaking—not out of fear, but in anticipation of what he might do.

***

It was fifteen minutes until a mandatory office-wide meeting. Finally, Sam saw an opportunity to get a word with Wendy, who had been elusive and busy throughout the day, working with the other assistants to personally raise funds for Raphael Sanchez's widow. He found her in her office, on the other side of the fourth floor, counting cash and change.

"Hey." Sam gently knocked on the already ajar door.

"Oh hey. Been meaning to see you today." Wendy brushed her hair aside and turned her head.

"So…"

"So what?"

Had Sam had his thunder stolen by a faulty pipe? A terrible thought to think, but he couldn't help but be irked his bold gesture of defiance was overshadowed.

"So…" he managed to get out. "How's the fundraising going?"

"Meh. Some serious cheapskates here," said Wendy.

"You said you wanted to see me?"

"I did."

"Yeah?"

"To donate. When I came by earlier you weren't there." Wendy swung around in her chair, now facing Sam. "I've hit up everyone but you and the creepy guy in inspections who only wears yellow ties."

That was it? She baited him to go after United and he did and now it was just going to end there? While unemployed last year, Sam caught an interview with Mariah Carey on one of those dopey afternoon shows where she complained how her film 'Glitter' tanked at the box office because it was released a week after 9/11. Was he coming off like that? Was this his Glitter?

"I'm good for fifty bucks," Sam said as he sat down beside her. He pulled out a checkbook and began scribbling.

"Wow, generous. Thank you," Wendy said, still all business.

Sam decided on the 'choose your own adventure' route, remaining vague and letting her bring it up. "So, what do you think of 'The Incident'?"

"Which one? The one I'm fundraising for, or the other one?"

"The email wasn't impulsive, if that's what you're thinking. At least it wasn't completely impulsive. It was more of a—"

"Stop talking."

Sam looked on, confused.

"You just don't get it. Last night I talked to you, like, for real, because we were outside of work."

"I'm sorry?"

"The walls here are paper mache, Keith is a one-man NSA. These types of things are meant to be discussed after work, is what I'm saying."

"You want to hang out outside of work?" Sam felt a trembling in his chest but tried to keep his face calm.

"Not on a date, or anything," said Wendy.

"No, of course not." Sam swallowed.

"Yeah. Keep in mind that I don't know you or trust you, but I also don't want you talking about these things out in the open, to me at work."

Sam shifted in his seat. "Last night you said I thought this town was shitty. I don't think that."

"No?"

"I'm very much on the fence. Was hoping a local of some sort could show me around. Point out the good food and places with good people."

"Okay. Maggie's Diner tomorrow at 6 p.m. And I don't mean to play up the cloak and dagger angle, but don't tell anyone. You got a giant target on your back and I don't want to be known as a woman who associates with…"

"Radicals?"

"I was gonna say malcontents who send company emails drunk at 1 a.m."

Sam stood up, unable to contain his grin. "Great. I'll see you there. Oh, and I wouldn't suggest cashing that until Thursday. Either that or tomorrow…"

"Don't worry, I can pay."

"Perfect." Sam backed out of the office. Caught up in their back and forth, he had completely forgotten Greg's warning about Wendy. But what harm could a single night out do?

Chapter 10

The mandatory office-wide meeting was to take place in the same conference fifth-floor room Sam had once been thrown out of. Five minutes before, Sam heard a knock on his door. When he saw it was Julie, he braced himself for "blessed morning" and a tidal wave of her latest "news." But it never came. Julie said nothing at all. Her usual flushed gregariousness had been replaced with something else. Her eyes were narrowed to sharp pieces of flint. She still said nothing, so Sam piped in, "Every-thing okay?"

"No, nothing is okay. How could things be okay? Our com-munity has been attacked." Sam hadn't known she was capable of speaking with such icy force.

"Yes. I agree, today has been really upsetting, but we still don't know the cause of the explosion. It seems premature—"

"Of course you would say that."

Sam got the sense he shouldn't follow up, but he couldn't help himself. "Look, if this is about the queries I sent, I'd be very happy to go over my reasoning and methodology, which I believe were quite standard."

"I'm not here to discuss methodology." She lingered on the last word mockingly. "Charlie sent me to make sure you come to this meeting."

Sam wanted to ask why Charlie would send a hostile escort to a meeting that he was obviously planning to go to, but for once, his hunch that silence would be wiser got the best of him.

After a silent walk and elevator ride with Julie, he took a seat at the table in the conference room and put his notepad and pen on the smooth oak. The triple J's sat directly across from him at the table—they had been murmuring softly, but the second Sam sat down they went silent. Wendy was in the far corner of the room, which was as packed as the Energy Conservation meeting, but this time somber as a synagogue. Keith, the inspector with a rural Missouri drawl, was sitting in a chair near the door. Sam lifted his hand in a quick hello, but Keith quickly averted his gaze, staring past at the wall behind Sam's head. Jesus, he's pretending not to see me, Sam thought. Sam spotted Greg in a chair against the wall, not far from Wendy. When their eyes met, Greg put his hands together and made a tossing motion, as if throwing a basketball. Sam tapped his fingers on the top of his own head and shot him a barely perceptible smile. When you're brand new and already the office outcast, best not to make any quick moves, Sam thought to himself. I wonder how long it's going to take for Wendy to hate me too.

Charlie walked into the room and sat at the head of the table closest to the door. A man followed close behind—he was tall and wearing an expensive suit the color of coal, pointed leather shoes protruding from beneath his slacks. It was Thomas French, the president of United Gas. What's he doing here? Sam wondered. Doesn't he have an investigation to cooperate with?

Another man walked in and closed the door behind him. He was tall and slim, hair coiffed back in a smooth dome that rose above his forehead. Sam winced. It was the man with the In-fraGard binder who had rushed him out of this same room.

The two men took a seat to Charlie's left and right. "Okay everyone, it's been quite a day," said Charlie, his voice booming with the authority of a commander-in-chief addressing a war room. "We're going to go over the facts as they pertain to the Commission. You're all aware United Gas has an ongoing rate case."

Everyone turned to look at Sam, including Mr. French, who wasn't trying to hide his sneer. Sam looked down at his hands, his face burning.

"Law enforcement has not yet determined the cause of the explosion, but terrorism has not been ruled out," Charlie continued.

Charlie touched his thumbs and forefingers together, forming a diamond with his hands. "No matter the cause of the explosion, we can learn from this incident about how we, as an agency, can use our unique position to better fight terrorism."

Wait, what? wondered Sam. If it's not something, how can it not being something help us prepare for that something?

"I'd like to introduce Ray Moore." Charlie gestured with his hands towards the tall, slim man with slicked back hair. "He's the FBI liaison who is coordinating the Central Illinois chapter of InfraGard." He paused, looking expectantly around the room. "Anyone want to describe this program? Wendy?"

She sat up straight in her chair and crossed her legs, her eyes brightening, a star pupil. "Sure," she said, with a brusque nod of her head. "InfraGard is a public-private partnership between the FBI and the business community to protect our nation's critical infrastructure: water systems, power grids, gas mains, the internet."

Sam was startled at how different her voice sounded, stripped of its usual bite. I can't wait to ask her more about this over dinner, Sam thought, the prospect of their non-date date sending warmth radiating through him.

"That's right," said Ray Moore. His voice was high and nasal—he reminded Sam of frat boys who'd gone to Northwestern straight from private school. "The best way to protect critical infrastructure is to work with its leaders. Businessmen like Mr. French are our eyes and ears."

Ray Moore paused and looked at the room, as if weighing each person's reaction so that he could enter it into a behavioral analysis database. He paused on Sam and, looking directly at him, said, "Since September 11, our network has become indispensable to national security."

Thomas French gave the same glassy smile he wore at the gala, as though he were handing the Commission a giant check, instead of the reverse. "We see our ongoing relationships with law enforcement and the local regulatory community as central to our ability to give back to our community. We hope to continue our mutually cooperative relationship."

Charlie tapped the knuckles of both hands on the table. "We received a tip from InfraGard I'm sharing with you—and no one else. We have reason to think a journalist has or will be reaching out to many of you in the wake of the explosion. You are to tell us immediately if this happens, no exceptions. We have reason to think this individual is conducting suspicious activity, and the flow of information here is critical."

"Who should we tell?" Keith sounded concerned.

Mr. Moore handed his business card around the room. "You

can come directly to me."

Sam wanted to ask where this "intelligence" came from, but he stopped himself, remembering Greg's warning. Instead he began writing in his notebook: "Journalist, second warning."

"We also want to review some new staff protocols," Charlie continued. "As some of you may know, it appears that Raphael Sanchez, sadly killed in this morning's explosion, was an illegal alien. We still don't know the cause of the explosion, but we view this as a wake-up call—not just for the school district, but for everyone in public service. We're concerned that this slipped through the cracks."

Charlie took a confessional tone. "To think someone could be working so closely with children, in proximity to a breach of our critical infrastructure, no less, and we didn't know he was breaking the law."

Sam couldn't stop himself. "I don't understand what Raphael's status has to do with anything. He's the victim."

Charlie raised his voice, a warning. "I know, and we are very saddened by his loss, but remember, every crisis is an opportunity. The point is not to disparage Mr. Sanchez, it's to use his death to deepen our protocols so in the event of a wide scale terrorist action we are prepared."

Keith eagerly chimed in, "I, for one, am grateful we now know there are holes in our immigration screening process. If something like this can tighten our procedures, then his death won't be in vain, you know?"

"Exactly." Charlie said.

"The legacy he would have wanted, surely," said Sam, leaning back in his chair.

Mr. French ignored Sam's potshot. "I'm sure you are all wondering what the company is doing to protect our critical infrastructure. We'll be co-hosting a seminar on updated security measures at our facility, in tandem with Eagle Security. Details will be forthcoming." Once again, that smile, as if to say, "You're welcome, but you owe me."

Sam remembered the man at the top of the guard tower, patting the eagle logo with his hand. Sam felt like he was up there now, peering over a vast expanse he was tasked with protecting, the harsh wind in his face, fighting the urge to scramble down the ladder. Sam looked over at Wendy—her star-student sparkle had dulled and she was a deflated balloon, leaning back in her chair, chin in her hands. Just thirty hours until dinner, thought Sam. I hope I can hold on until then.

***

The next morning, Dee Dee put out her hand as Sam walked past her desk. "Charlie wants you to go to a thing today. A brown bag at the Hilton hotel." Dee Dee wasn't looking at him, just staring at her own hand, which lingered in the air between them.

"What's it about?"

"Private-public partnerships, something like that."

"He wants me to do that now—with everything happening?"

"It was scheduled weeks ago, before the explosion, and Charlie thinks it's important we go on with business as usual. 'Springfield Together' is our motto." She said this phrase with extra bite, as though Sam had intentionally violated it.

"Okay. Where is the brown bag?"

"The Hilton. It's the tallest building in town, even you can't miss it."

At 11:45 Sam walked the four blocks to the hotel. The wind blew heavy drops of cold rain into his face. He walked into the lobby of the Hilton, which was decorated in a soft, carpeted '70s theme, and ran his fingers through his hair, shaking the water onto the floor. A short man with a goatee standing behind the desk gave him a scowl.

Sam walked in the opposite direction along the industrial gray carpet and saw a large, professionally-printed cardboard sign that perched on a black easel. "Harnessing the power of public-private partnerships," it said, the bottom littered with corporate logos. Sam scanned them for United Gas. Sure enough it was there—a navy-blue capital U with a lower-case g, above an image of two hands shaking. Prairie Water was next to it, illustrated with a single blade of prairie grass.

Sam followed a series of hand-drawn arrows taped to the wall down a hallway and through a tall oak door. When he pushed it open he was hit with a buzz of talking and laughter. The large room, which appeared to be perfectly square, was divided into small, circular tables, each holding six chairs. On the side opposite the door, a slide projector was beaming onto a screen an image of two people in a kayak, white water cascading and spraying around them. Their expressions were resolute as they deftly pressed their oars into the water.

Sam walked to a long table by the window on the left of the room and grabbed a brown bag. He scanned the room for someone he recognized. It was a sea of bald spots, beige suits, and American flag lapel-pins. Keith was in the far corner, poking at what looked like a soggy bologna sandwich. In the center of the room, at a table facing the screen, Sam saw Wendy's unmistakable chestnut hair.

Sam sat at a half empty table in the corner of the room opposite Keith, nodding hello to a man on the other side who looked up at him with a smile. He emptied the contents of his bag, skipping past the mystery sandwich, and reached straight for the chocolate chip cookie. It was surprisingly soft and chewy.

Just as Sam was reaching for a crumb that had fallen onto the table, the lights went off, the picture of the kayakers illuminating the room. Sam saw the shadow of a man walk to the front. Had he entered through a side door? Was this a David Bowie concert? The room went silent.

A booming voice—amplified by a microphone—filled the room. "The waters are rushing around you, threatening to suck you under. The roar is deafening."

Sam's mouth felt dry, the cookie mush sticking to the insides of his cheeks. He recognized that voice. It was Phil. Can I go anywhere in this town without running into him? Sam wondered.

"Your survival depends on maintaining perfect balance—and absolute trust," Phil shouted out through the darkness. "Each man rows for the other and for himself. Each is the other's best protection from the cascade and boulders that await. This," Phil paused, "is the absolute partnership."

At this, the lights flipped on. Phil was standing in the front of the room, a small, black microphone pinned to his collar, his eyes wide, like a child telling scary stories around a campfire.

Sam saw a young woman in business professional clothing run up to the slide projector. She slipped in an image that just read, "Springfield Together." Sam saw Keith, across the room, somberly nod his head.

"As we all know, Springfield has suffered a horrible tragedy," said Phil. "Our co-investigation with local law enforcement, the FBI, and the governor's office is the ultimate private-public partnership. And our public safety depends on it."

Phil paused as the young woman went to the projector again, and this time a single word appeared on the screen in neon-green lettering against a black background: "BIAS."

Phil walked towards the crowd, his fingers laced together. "Do we think of the government and the private sector as partners? One of the things that makes trust so difficult is that our vision is clouded with bias. Our bias says that the private sector will always be money grubbing profit-seekers, the government will always be a bureaucratic roadblock, we will always be the worst versions of ourselves in the other's eyes, and we will never come together to solve complex problems."

Phil took one step closer to the crowd, so that he was only about three feet from the table where Wendy was sitting. His hands were at his side as he surveyed the room. "I've only got you for one hour, so I'm going to ask you to count off by threes and divide into groups. Each group will be asked to discuss one of these words—trust, reliability, and credibility—and what it means to you."

The room of about fifty counted off then descended into brief chaos as they migrated to their respective places. When Sam got to the "credibility" corner, he saw Wendy standing there. He tried to catch her eye with a sardonic, knowing expression, but when she looked back at him, she just seemed tired.

The group circled up, and Sam noticed Keith was standing a few people over. Sam felt a firm palm on his back. He turned around and Phil's shiny head of hair practically whacked him in the face.

"Oh, uh, hi," said Sam.

"Glad you could make it." Phil's teeth were impossibly white when he smiled.

His hand still on Sam's shoulder, Phil maneuvered—or did he shove—Sam over to the right so that he could join the circle. Phil projected his voice towards its center. "I'll be facilitating this break-out group. Let's go around the circle, say who we are, and what credibility means to you."

"I'll start." Of course, it was Keith, standing a few people down from Wendy, wearing a white dress shirt tucked into brown pants. "I'm Keith Landrey, inspections at the Illinois Commerce Commission. What does credibility mean to me?" He crossed his arms in front of him. "Credibility means you do what you say you will. You show up. You lead." Keith was all warmth to the group, but somehow managed to avoid Sam's eyes.

"Great, that's great." Phil nodded authoritatively and Sam looked around the circle. A few heads nodded in agreement, others looked politely bored, Wendy among them. Next up was a young executive assistant for the head of Arnold Construction, his hair carefully spiked, who said credibility means your actions having the same positive outcome again and again. After him, a woman from the health department, Sam couldn't make out which role. Her face seemed kind and worn. "Credibility means you have a good reputation."

Surely Phil didn't think these platitudes were actually useful.

The room was silent. Everyone was looking at Sam. "Your turn," Phil said into his ear.

"Oh, hi. I'm Sam Golden from the Illinois Commerce Commission. And I, uh, pass."

112

"Come on, why don't you give it a try?" said Phil.

"No, really, I'm okay."

"This is a judgment-free zone," Phil pressed.

Sam looked deep into Phil's eyes, trying to connect to the version of this man he used to know—or thought he knew. "I'm good."

Phil put his hand back on Sam's shoulder. "Come on, old buddy. Give it a go."

"No really, old buddy. I pass."

"Cat got your tongue?"

"I'm just listening."

"This is a partnership. You can't take but not give."

Sam let a single chuckle escape his throat. "Believe me, passing is a gift."

"Sam, please. You're holding us up." It was Wendy, standing across the circle, her feet spread apart about the same distance as her shoulders, hands at her side. Her long bangs were partially in her face, and the eye that peaked out looked exasperated. Sam thought about the dinner they were supposed to have later that night, Greg's warning a faint refrain.

"I, uh, okay," said Sam. He cleared his throat. "Credibility means doing things you don't want to do if it helps the group."

Phil, his smile magnanimous. "Now you're getting the hang of it."

***

The rain had stopped, and Sam biked carefully around puddles to Maggie's Diner, hoping to avoid sporting a fresh racing stripe of brown water down his back. There was no bike rack out front—or seemingly anywhere in this town—so he locked it to a stop sign.

Sam saw a homemade sign taped to the door. In large black lettering, it said, "Springfield Together, 11/02/02" and beneath it, "Raphael Sanchez, R.I.P." They got that up quickly, Sam thought to himself.

Sam spotted Wendy sitting at a booth by the window, her face amber in the glow of a neon orange "open" sign. Voices blared from four large televisions hovering over the bar to Sam's left, and old photographs of Route 66 decorated the walls.

"Wouldn't it be weird if someone from work saw us here?" said Sam, as he sat on a wooden chair, its back digging into his shoulder blades.

Wendy swatted at the air between them. "Not a chance. This place is too low-brow for them."

"I think it's nice." Sam put the thin paper napkin on his lap, glad that he'd remembered to do that, and leaned his elbows on the table, which looked like it had just been scrubbed with Shout.

"Wait until you try the horseshoe. I already ordered one for you," Wendy said.

"The what?"

"Only Springfield's world-famous culinary specialty." Her eyes were bright, just like earlier in the meeting, but now there was a spark of mischief. Can she turn it on and off? Sam wondered.

"Well I'm in the right place," said Sam. "So…"

"So what?"

"I know it's a horrible cliché but I have to ask, who was that guy last night?"

"Sam…"

"He just seemed wholly uninterested in helping us out with the papers and I wanted to make sure you're not consorting with a serial killer."

"I can assure you he's—"

"Callousness towards the helpless and weak is an early sign."

"That so?"

"I read it in Newsweek."

"You're helpless and weak?"

"After four beers, yes."

Wendy's expression turned sad. "Sam, you didn't have to do what you did last night, sending that email to half the city." She had lowered her voice.

Sam leaned back and crossed his arms. "You think I did that because of you?"

Before Wendy could respond, a short busser who looked to be in his early twenties with cropped hair and a worn, green t-shirt placed a plate in front of each of them. As he was walking away, Sam looked closer at the back of his t-shirt. In faded black letters, it said, "1999 Healthy Futures Scholarship winner."

"Did you see that guy's shirt?" asked Sam.

"No. Why?"

"It says he won the Healthy Futures award."

"Oh—good for him."

"I just went to their gala. Strange coincidence."

"Yeah."

Sam hadn't touched his food yet. "Why would he be working here bussing tables if he won some big scholarship?"

"I don't know. Anyway, your food's getting cold."

Sam looked down at a plate heaping with fries smothered in bright orange cheese sauce that looked like it had to be composed of at least 40 percent plastic. He poked with his fork and found, beneath the pile, a piece of soggy white bread topped with a beef patty.

"I think my cholesterol went up just looking at this."

Wendy laughed. "It's a great cure for hangovers. But the problem is it also gives you a hangover."

"An amazing piece of Springfield culture. You're, uh, from here?"

"Unfortunately, yes."

"And you say I'm the snob?"

"Well, if you grew up in this town and stayed, it generally means you have no money."

"Moving all the time can mean the same. My debt collectors literally don't know where to find me."

Sam picked up a cheesy fry with his fork and gingerly put it in his mouth. "What you said on the street the other night, it's not that I dislike Springfield or the people in it, it's just, I don't want to get too attached since, if my history is any guide, I won't be here long."

"Ah yes, a rolling stone."

"The strangest thing happened the other night. I don't have a key for my apartment door because my landlord is kind of a scatterbrain, but she eventually got me one. But when she tried to hand it to me I just... froze."

"Over a key?"

"The key chain had these big block letters, 'Home of Lincoln,' and it just seemed to me that once I had it, it was real."

"Like it was a sign of your commitment?"

"It's stupid, I know. In my mind I'm still in Chicago living another life."

Wendy put down her fork and looked at Sam. "What are you trying to do?"

"Avoid choking on this pile of lard."

"I mean, with the United case."

"I don't know. I think the most I can do is make people's lives a little better, offer an extra layer of protection."

"What if you get fired first?"

Sam pierced the patty with his fork and cut it with his knife. It felt rubbery, unlike the bread, which was as soft as mulch. "You think they're going to fire me?"

"They're already trying to. But you're so new, they haven't built a file yet. They can't make it look like retaliation." She paused, picked at her own patty. "I shouldn't be telling you this."

Sam exhaled.

"But it's not too late," continued Wendy. "Phil said—"

"You talk to Phil?" asked Sam.

"Apparently you do too."

"We were in Seattle around the same time, got caught up in activism together—and after things went bad, we stopped talking." Wendy didn't say anything. It was as if she already knew.

"Anyway, I know what Phil wants me to do," Sam added.

Wendy bent forward. "For God's sake, they're leaning on the dead janitor's poor wife, what's-her-name, about her being un-documented, trying to get her to not talk to the press, to go along with the, you know, story."

"What, it's an inside job now?" He let out a grin.

Wendy didn't smile back. "They're looking at a major lawsuit, Sam. But listen..."

"Right," Sam cut in, "but so long as it's terrorism, or people suspect it could be, we're not talking about delayed maintenance schedules, deferred upgrades, lack of reinvesting in safety tech. We're talking about higher fences and background checks and information sharing. The whole goddamn thing is a multitool, good for whatever."

"Look, they don't—"

"They? You keep saying 'they.' *They*'re leaning on the widow, *they* could get sued. I can't tell where United ends and the FBI and Eagle Security begin. Did 'they' fire that guy from inspections?"

Sam felt a pang of tenderness as he watched Wendy take a breath and collect herself. "There's a journalist, a journalist who's asking questions," said Wendy. "Has she contacted you?"

"I'm sorry?" Sam wondered why she'd suddenly shifted focus.

"Has a journalist contacted you?"

Sam held his fork in midair. Was this the real purpose of her dinner invitation?

"Funny enough, no." Sam stared straight at Wendy, hoping he seemed convincing.

"Hum. Surprising. She's been contacting everyone. Did you check your email in the past few hours?"

119

Why wouldn't Wendy drop it? Sam's stomach suddenly felt heavy. How much potato and cheese had he ingested to enjoy the company of a woman who was just looking for information to help her boss? Or was she? Maybe he was being paranoid. After all, she had warned him that his job was at risk. But were her warnings, her veiled indictments of United, calculated to win his trust? For the first time, Sam looked over at the television. He caught a glimpse of a reporter at the school, before the scene cut away to a breaking bulletin about a police officer who had saved a kitten from a tree.

Sam looked down at his hands, resting on the edge of the table, then back at Wendy. "Why are you so interested in the reporter?"

Wendy half opened her mouth like she was about to say something, then shut it. "So, seeing Phil again? Must be wild for you."

"Phil?" Confusion flashed across Sam's face. Why was she diverting from his question?

"Knowing someone when they were radical and seeing them turn into Phil. I've only known this Phil. I'm having a hard time imagining him throwing tear gas back at cops."

"'Wild' is one way of putting it. He really did a 180, but in retrospect it's not a total shock. One day we show up to a meeting, to plan for a major shutdown, and poof—he's gone. Then I see him a few years later and he's this hotshot corporate guy. Makes you wonder."

Wendy ran her fingers through her hair, brushing it away from her forehead, exposing rows of faint wrinkles. "I don't have access to his file 'cause he's at United. But people talk—it's a small town."

"So I've noticed."

"Word is, he wasn't a snitch if that's what you were imply-
ing. He was a scared kid, got arrested and they offered him a
clean slate if *he did* snitch, but he took ninety days in jail instead.
Came out and his parents put him up at a job at United—his father's cousin or something. That or they'd cut him off."

"Yeah, well, not everyone has that safety net."

"But if you did, would you have turned your nose up at it?"

Sam stared back with a blank expression, not wanting to let
her know he wasn't sure. He had to admit there were a lot of
things he wasn't sure of. Why had she been so quick to defend
Phil? And why the deflection about that journalist? Greg's warning echoed in his head, even if he didn't want it to be true. Wendy was a shock of fuchsia among dim shades of grey and white.
He wasn't ready to turn away from how she filled him with a
dreadful sense of aliveness, a feeling of being in motion, even if
she was bad news. Torn between the urge to protect himself and
the desire to continue following this thread, Sam knew which
choice he'd make. It was pre-determined the second she walked
into that fourth floor meeting. He noticed Wendy was looking
down at her phone, holding it just below the table line.

"Oh, uh, you need to take that?" he mumbled.

"Actually, I—" When she looked at him, her expression was
a twist of anger and worry. "I'm sorry, I have to go."

"Oh, that's fine."

"Yeah, I just…" she trailed off.

"It's okay," said Sam. "You don't have to explain." He
paused. "You know what, let me pay, please. While I still have a

job. You should go."

"Thank you," she said, as she put her phone in her purse and snapped it shut. When she stood up to put her coat on, Sam noticed she'd barely made a dent in her horseshoe, which was steaming in the fluorescent lighting.

As he watched her walk through the restaurant, then push open the door, a branch quivered in his chest. Well, it's clear I like her, he thought to himself. And that I'd be an idiot to trust her.

Chapter 11

The funeral for Raphael Louis Sanchez Jr. was scheduled two days later—Charlie had sent around an email saying anyone who wanted to attend would be excused. Sam wore his suit to work and, at noon, walked a mile to the Holy Sacrament Parish, its sharp steeple jutting through a maze of telephone wires. Inside, a painted wood carving of Jesus on the cross, his arms outstretched, faced a coffin draped in white cloth. Sam willed the floor not to creak as he sat a few rows back from the crowd, which was large enough to fill half the pews.

"With this water we call to mind Raphael Sanchez's baptism." The priest's voice seemed to ricochet off of the domed ceiling. Sam saw the back of a woman's head in the front row, her arms around two children whose heads barely reached above the back of the pew. Even from twenty pews back, Sam could see her shoulders heaving. An old woman in the row behind her placed a hand on the woman's back and held it there as she patted her own face with a handkerchief.

Behind the family was a crowd of kids, probably high school age, leaning their heads against each other's shoulders and hugging their knees. Clustered around them were about a dozen men and women who looked like they each had a good twenty years of hard manual labor behind them. Some of them seemed to know the kids. Sam wondered if they were sanitation workers from the high school. In the back, Sam recognized the police chief from television, but he didn't see anyone else from the Commission.

When the priest began a call and response, Sam stared straight ahead. He'd grown more comfortable in churches, but the one thing he would never do is pray. "And let perpetual light shine upon him," the room answered in unison. A female voice came from behind Sam, where he thought no one was. He turned around and saw Allison, the journalist, walking down the aisle in his direction. When she saw him, she stopped, looked around the room, then walked to the pew behind him and sat down.

Sam kept his gaze fixed in front of him as the crowd answered the priest, "In the land of the living."

Allison leaned forward and whispered into Sam's ear. "You're the only one who shows up."

Sam said nothing.

"And let our cry come unto thee," the room said in unison.

"Do you think those are his students and coworkers?" Allison whispered again.

After a few beats of silence, Sam whipped to the right, giving Allison a glimpse of his profile. "I assume so," he whispered.

A man in his early forties walked up to the pulpit and leaned into a microphone. "I can't tell you how grateful we are that all of you came out for my little brother," he said softly.

"This whole thing reeks and you know it," Allison pressed. Sam said nothing. "United," she continued whispering, "they've been putting off proper maintenance for decades, prioritizing dividends to their execs and investor friends and eventually, given enough time and wear and tear and the immutable laws of entropy, it was gonna catch up to them. But 9/11 bought them time. An influx of cash from the feds to fight al Qaeda and shore up critical infrastructure—this put a band-aid on the problem and made questioning them unpatriotic. Information requests dry up overnight and suddenly, reporters got bigger problems. But, as evidenced by our sitting here at Holy Sacrament, this War on Terror can only buy time, not stop the inevitable."

Sam kept looking forward. "If you know so much, what do you need me for?" He said it more softly this time, scanning the room to see if anyone had noticed them talking.

"I'm a reporter, I can't report theories, only facts. That's where you come in." Sam turned around to look at Allison. She wrote something on a piece of paper and handed it to him. "I'll be here after. It's right around the corner."

Just then, Sam saw Thomas French enter the room and walk slowly down the aisle. Sam scrambled to the end of the pew then stood against the wall, as Thomas French took his seat on the other side of the aisle. Raphael's brother walked down from the podium, his head bowed, hands clasped behind him. Sam slowly and carefully folded the piece of paper, so as not to make any noise, and placed it in his pocket.

When the service was over, Sam walked as rapidly as he could down the aisle, short of breaking into a trot. Did Thomas French see me talking to her? he worried to himself. Allison could stand to be a little more discreet. Just as he pressed his hand against the tall arched door leading outside, Sam heard someone calling his name. He turned around. Angelo. He was wearing a navy-blue suit with a gray tie.

"I barely recognize you in that suit," said Sam.

"I can't say the same, since it's the only suit I've seen you wear."

Sam held out his hand, and Angelo gave it a hearty shake, then held it a moment longer than Sam was expecting.

"What are you doing here?" asked Angelo.

"I don't know," said Sam. "Thought I should be here. It was a United gas line. And I'm on—"

"The United case. I know." Angelo paused. "Raphael was in our union, you know? We're demanding answers. They're ignoring us now, talking about auditing everyone's immigration status—it has a lot of people scared."

"Yeah?"

"But they can't shut us up. Not for long. The union is pissed off."

"You knew him?

"Raphael? Met him at a barbeque last August. Can't cook worth a damn. He put too much lighter fluid on the grill and almost singed my eyebrows off. But he's a funny guy—was a funny guy. Cute kids, too. Fucking shame, the whole thing."

Sam could see the crowd starting to exit the building, but Angelo wasn't done. "We're just a photo op to these people. But we're everywhere. They ignore us but we have people in all the government buildings. Anyway, it's good of you to be here."

"Please don't say that," said Sam. "There's nothing good about this."

"His family appreciates it," said Angelo. "I know they do."

"Well, I hope they're okay," said Sam. "I'm so sorry for your loss." He gave Angelo's hand one more squeeze and pushed open the door just as the crowd moved towards him. He put a hand over his eyes to block the sunlight and ran down the stairs.

***

Allison was waiting for Sam in the same cafe he'd gone to with Wendy and Keith on the way back from the water sanitation facility. He ordered a hot chocolate from the barista, her hair orange this time, then sat down.

"You came!" The last vowel was long and flat—that curious mix of Midwestern and Southern drawl common in Central Illinois.

"This has to be totally anonymous, off the record, whatever the term is."

"No problem," said Allison, putting down the pen she had been holding. "I won't even take notes." She paused. "You have no idea how long I've been trying to get an analyst to talk to me."

"Your specificity implies you have non-analysts from the Commission talking to you."

Allison set down her cup of coffee. "You came to a One Springfield meeting. No one ever does. And you were there today. Why?"

"I'm not sure. I thought I should be there. I'm on the United rate case, but you already know that. What about you? Were you hoping I would show up?"

"No. I've been on this case a while. I thought I should pay my respects." Allison shook her head, her gaze lifting to the back wall. "He must have been really loved. All those students."

"Yeah." Sam cupped both hands around his drink. "What is this 'case?'"

"Two years ago, after I read about those gas line explosions in Boston—you may have heard of them—I figured I'd reach out to the Commission for the safety inspection reports here. Due diligence for a local journalist. But they blew me off, didn't respond to my phone calls or my emails, and just turned me away when I showed up at the office."

Sam nodded once. "Shocking."

"So then I submitted a FOIA request, but months later that was rejected on the grounds that it was overly burdensome. My follow-up request, much narrower, was rejected too. So I tried again."

Sam interrupted. "Who did you say you work for? The Springfield Weekly?"

Allison rolled her eyes and gave a quick flick of her head, as if to discard Sam's comment. "We may be a rag, but we're all this town's got as far as alt weeklies go. Besides, my editor used to be a big shot at the Tribune."

She continued, "In October of 2001, I tried again. But this time, their logic had changed. They said releasing safety inspection information could pose a national security threat, because then the terrorists would get access to the floor plans of 'critical infrastructure' facilities." Allison let out a sharp laugh.

"That sounds like something Keith would say."

"Keith?"

"Just this guy from inspections."

"Well I have no idea who I was dealing with. It was like *The Bourne Identity*. I could never contact them directly. I would reach out to them on a comment page and they would send cryptic emails from the company account. They were real pros at telling me to get lost."

"Well, I bet you'll get what you're looking for now. A lot of people are going to be asking for those reports."

"I'm afraid that doesn't mean they'll get them—at least not in time."

"In time for what?"

"Who knows." Allison looked at Sam. "Do you know anything at all about the inspections? Have you seen any reports?"

"I haven't."

"But you're the analyst on the United case."

"I know. It doesn't make me look very good."

"I've been talking with people—One Springfield, the janitors' union—they want to see the reports too. This isn't going to die down, Sam. A man is dead. His coworkers want to know what happened."

Allison's eyes were burning now. "If you could get me anything, Sam. A single report. An email. I'll never share your name."

"They'd know it was me."

"Well if they knew, so would the family of Raphael Sanchez. And they'd be grateful." Allison paused. "If you give me something, I'll show you what I have."

"The non-analyst?"

"Give me something solid and we can work together," Allison said. "Until then, I don't know whether you're a corporate spook working me over."

Sam was about to burst with indignation but stopped and thought it over. She's right, what had he offered other than hand-wringing? "Alright, Fair enough. Two-way street and so forth."

"And so forth." Allison leaned in. "Look Sam, I want to trust you, but you've been in this town for all of five minutes and I'm gonna need you to ante up."

Sam exhaled. "At least tell me who turned you away when you asked for safety reports. If I know this I can use my access at the Commission to follow up for you, for us."

"Cute, there's an 'us' now," Allison smirked. "I only have the person's employee ID number. I haven't been able to figure out who it belongs to, and no one will answer my questions." She tore off a piece of paper, wrote a number on it, and handed it to Sam. He folded it and put it in his pocket.

***

The walk back to the office was cold, the sky the same colorless grey as Sam's breath. He thought of Raphael's wife and children. It had been so long since he'd seen his own family. He wondered what his mother was doing now. Probably sitting on her couch, wrapped in a shawl, reading mystery novels next to a fireplace that was never filled with fire. For a moment, Sam felt a fierce ache for the Stamford woods, the stone walls he practiced his balance on as a child until he could run along their edges.

Sam balled his hands into yellow-knuckled fists as he quickened his pace, a thin layer of sweat gathering on his lower back, his jaw clenched. Back at the office, he bounded up the stairs, past the security guard, and through the hallway. As if riding the crest of a wave, he went past Dee Dee on her phone, past the triple J's clustered in the hallway, and landed at Greg's door, where he gave three knocks.

"That inspector, the one who left," Sam said, standing in front of Greg's desk.

Greg took a long look at Sam. "Yeah."

"Do you know how to get in touch with him?"

"Sam, I'm not—"

"Please. No one will know it was you. I won't drag you into this."

Greg hesitated for a moment and then, just as Sam knew he would, reached for his rolodex and handed over a yellowed card with a number and an address on it.

Sam held it tightly in his right hand and with his other hand, reached into his pocket, pulled out the piece of paper Allison had given him, with the employee ID number of whoever had told her to get lost. He put it on Greg's desk. "Sorry, just one more thing. Whose employee ID is this?"

Greg unfolded the paper. "Where did you get this?"

"It doesn't matter. I just need to know." At Greg's suddenly stony look, Sam paused, thinking he'd gone too far. "Actually, don't worry about it. I can ask Dee Dee."

"No, it's okay. I can look it up for you." Greg stared at his computer, typing and moving the mouse in small circles as he clicked with his forefinger. Two minutes passed in silence before Greg said, "Ah, I found it. That's Wendy's employee ID."

"Wendy? Are you sure?"

Sam put a hand against the wall, steadying himself. It was Wendy who had stonewalled Allison.

"Positive. Sam, is something wrong?"

What surprised Sam the most was how unsurprised he actually was. It all made sense now: She wasn't flirting, she was disarming. Put the doddering new guy on the United case and watch him closely—sic the charming office babe on him. He always thought she was far too clever to be Charlie's assistant. Now he knew what her real job was, and it made him feel like a dope.

After a beat of self-pity and anger, he couldn't resist a creeping feeling there was more to the story. Was it his crush or his instinct for bullshit? A smile like that was impossible to fake, he thought. Sam knew he had a knack for conscious self-delusion—indeed, it was a requirement of all socialists: knowing the odds against our better angels were long but worth betting on anyway. Maybe Wendy was decent after all, maybe her affections were sincere. Maybe she was pressured into it. Maybe she had her own reasons.

"Sam?" Greg interrupted. He'd been standing in silence for a good half minute. "Everything okay?"

"Yes." He snatched the file from Greg's desk and began darting for the door. "I gotta go see about an old case."

Chapter 12

Sam ran around the corner, so focused he didn't notice the hard pellets of rain until they dripped down his forehead into his eyes. He pulled out his phone and, shielding it with his other hand, dialed the number. But it was disconnected. The inspector's name, Isaac Jones, would surely turn up too many entries in the Yellow Pages. There was only one thing left to do.

Sam simply left, like he'd seen Charlie do so many early afternoons and, like Charlie, he waved to Dee Dee on the way out. "A meeting," he mouthed as she talked on the phone, and she gave him a nod. Sam rode his bike under wide shadows of clouds, a thin ribbon of robin's egg blue at the horizon. The rain had let up, but puddles sent water streaming up his back, and he knew the back of his only suit would be splattered with muck by the time he got to the East Side.

The house was on an unremarkable block, its stoop decorated with potted plants, exterior the color of butter. Sam rang the doorbell, but no one came. He rubbed his hands together and then held them to his face, his breath forming small clouds.

He tried again, but still no one. So he knocked hard, imagining the sound echoing through an empty house. About thirty seconds later he heard footsteps. And then someone opened the door a crack, but not enough to see who was on the other side.

"Can I help you?" The voice belonged to a woman who did not seem like she was in the mood to help anyone.

"I'm looking for Isaac Jones."

"He doesn't live here anymore." The woman closed the door.

Sam knocked again, this time lightly. "Sorry to bother you, but could I have a minute of your time? I'm from the Commerce Commission."

The door flew wide open. A woman who couldn't have been more than twenty-five was standing with a baby on one hip, her eyes furious. She was slender, probably just over five feet, with tight braids that reached just past her shoulders.

"What do you want with my father?"

"I'm sorry to intrude. I know it must be weird having a random white guy show up at your house."

"It's weird having a random any kind of guy show up to my house."

"Right, of course. This is the only way I knew to find him, is the thing."

"Well he's not here, thanks to y'all." The woman was speaking with forced constraint, and Sam saw the baby was undisturbed—smiling widely.

"I'm so sorry. That's what I want to ask about."

The child let out a giggle, then lunged for Sam's nose. He

smiled as he jerked his head away to avoid the baby's touch. "How old?" he asked.

The woman looked Sam up and down with an expression that wavered between skepticism and pity. Sam knew he probably looked like a stray cat, his hair stringy and flat from the rain. But maybe this woman is the kind who helps strays.

"She's nine months. You rode your bike here?"

"From Sixth and Capitol."

"What is it you say you do?"

"I'm a rate analyst. Brand new."

The woman said nothing.

"I'm on the United Gas case and I'm unsettled by some things and I—I want to know what happened with your father," Sam blurted out.

The woman put her hand on the door, probably to shut it in his face, Sam thought. But to his surprise, she opened it wider and stepped aside, gesturing with her arm. "Alright, come in. My name is Tiana."

They sat on folding chairs around a plastic table, and Tiana handed Sam a cup of Swiss Miss. He took a big gulp, letting the chunks of powder dissolve in his mouth, as the warmth made his fingers tingle. Across from him, Tiana held the baby on her knee, which never stopped bouncing. Before Sam knew what was happening he was telling her everything—about the testimony, InfraGard, the conversation with Allison. He knew if he was caught discussing confidential information with someone outside the Commission it would get him fired, but he had the feeling he could trust this woman.

With each piece of information, Tiana nodded encouragingly, but her expression turned to sympathy when he described the dinner with Wendy. "Am I being paranoid?" he asked, realizing he hadn't mentioned his suspicions of Wendy to anyone yet, not even Greg.

"I don't know," she said, but the expression in her eyes made it seem like she did.

By now, Tiana had softened to him, and Sam was emboldened to ask again what had happened to her dad. Tiana's tone was as matter-of-fact as a court stenographer reading back dialogue. "My father was an inspector. His training is in engineering. That's what he was paid to do. When he reported the condition of United's gas lines, he was told, 'Thank you very much, we'll take it from here.' And when they did nothing, he asked questions."

Tiana paused. When she spoke again, her voice was trembling. "My father was never aggressive or unprofessional."

"What did he see?"

"What did he see? Exactly what you expect. Why else would you ride your bike all the way here?" Tiana laughed for a moment, then stopped herself.

"Those gas lines are a mess," she said. "They are not safe, and United knows it. And so does the Commission."

The final sip of hot chocolate burned on the way down.

Tiana's matter-of-fact tone was gone. "It makes me so mad, because they'll never pay for what they did. But my dad had to move to a whole new city, whole new state. After the things they said about him, no one would hire him. They chased him out of town, not a small price to pay, given that I'm his only family. He had to move all the way to Madison to have any hope of salvaging his career. And even then, he had to start over, spent a few months waiting tables to get by."

"They were able to do that to him? But how…" Sam's voice trailed off. Where can I run to? The Commerce Commission was supposed to be his start-over. During college, Sam spent his summers back in Connecticut working at a garment factory in Norwalk. It was his job to cut pockets, and he was paid by the piece. He could still feel the dull panic as he raced the clock to produce enough to make a decent wage, and yet willed that second hand to move faster so he could go home. Ten minutes felt like an eternity, but somehow the time was always too short, or his hands too clumsy, to cut enough. That job, no doubt, would be waiting for him, along with a bed in his old room.

When Tiana responded, she startled Sam out of his reverie. "Everyone in this town who's in a position to hire knows each other. And when something goes wrong they cover each other's asses as if they were their own. They all golf together, and dine together, and donate to each other's causes. My dad, in his older years, he's gotten a bit naive."

"How's that?"

"He doesn't say it, but he does things, weird things, that make me think he thinks it'll all blow over, that he'll come back. He still has his mail forwarded here, he still pays a YMCA membership every month—including a locker, which isn't cheap— like he's just on a long vacation. I love him of course, but after six months it's just denial, you know?"

Sam paused. "Do you think your dad would talk to me?"

"Not possible." Tiana's voice grew quieter. "They made him sign an NDA. His lips are sealed or they'll sue him for the measly five grand they gave him on the way out. In fact, I'm not supposed to be talking to you, my dad said not to open the door for any of y'all."

Sam could have stopped there, but he thought of Allison's question, the look in her eyes. "Did he ever write any of his complaints about the Commission down?"

"That was his job."

Sam's heart quickened. "Do you know how I could get my hands on any documentation at all?"

"Why?"

"I think I want to try to do something about it." Sam was surprised to hear himself say those words, and was not entirely sure if he meant them.

The baby began softly whimpering, and Tiana stood up and bounced her on her shoulder. Once the baby quieted, Tiana spoke in a sing-song voice. "If you find anything and anyone asks about it later, you tell them you stole it from me."

"Stole it? Yes."

"I don't want those United lawyers shoving that NDA up our asses, and if you took the documents without my knowing, they can't. Understand?"

"Understood. Thank you so much."

The garage smelled like dust and rain, and about twelve boxes formed a small hill on the opposite side. "If the files are at this house, this is where you'll find them, along with all the other stuff he left behind." The baby's soft whimpers crescendoed into long wails, followed by gasping.

"I've got to put her down. Good luck." Tiana walked out and shut the door behind her.

Sam walked to the pile of boxes, each marked in black sharpie. "Clothes." "Books." "Photographs." At the foot of the pile was a black suitcase, on top of it, a bright blue gym bag. In the suitcase, 1970s clothes that Sam speculated Isaac would never wear again but couldn't part with. Sam always found it funny how much people held onto fashion from their "peak" years. In the gym bag, exactly what he expected: worn out running shoes, pool goggles, a small locker key, a rolled-up towel.

Sam walked to the other side of the pile, where there was just about a foot between the boxes and the wall. More books and clothes. This man left a lot behind, Sam thought to himself.

Sam saw a small box, a few feet away from the pile. He walked over but couldn't find a label.

He carefully tore off the tape and opened the box. A photo album with a single picture on the front—a man, smiling, in a graduation gown, holding a baby in one arm, his other slinked around the waist of a young woman, her head resting on his shoulder. He picked up the album and gently put it aside. He found a child's sticker book, a journal, and then—beneath that—an unmarked manila envelope.

He sat down on the ground and gently unclasped the envelope, emptying the contents onto his lap. But the pages that fell out were rejection letters for job applications. From St. Louis, Michigan, Alaska. Sam felt the stack. There must be forty in there. I'm not the only one, he thought, remembering the bitter gratitude that someone had taken the time to mail him a note on the company's letterhead, carefully signed, telling him he wasn't the right fit.

Sam put the contents back in the box and reached for the next one. It was roughly the size of a file cabinet. This could be it. But when Sam pulled the tape off, releasing the flaps, plumes of dust flew up from a stack of old records. He ran his fingers along them. Muddy Waters. The Beatles. Leadbelly.

Sam shut the flaps and pulled the dusty tape over them, sealing them closed. He reached for a box of a similar size, expecting it to be records, but when he tore it open, there was a binder resting at the top. When Sam opened it, he saw a stack of files. The first was labeled "Commerce Commission." But when he pulled out its contents, he just found an acceptance letter.

Sam thumbed through to see what the other files were named. "Insurance." "W-2s." When he saw one labeled "Inspection reports" he felt light and heavy at once, as if underwater. But when he reached into the file, there was nothing there. Why was every work file here except the inspection reports? he wondered. Couldn't just be a coincidence, could it?

Sam did a 360-degree scan of the garage then let out a deep breath. He had come up empty. As he stood, Tiana opened the garage door.

"Don't worry, I'm leaving soon," Sam said.

"I think it's great what you're trying to do, it's just, the baby…"

"I understand. Just one more thing: Earlier you said you weren't supposed to talk to any of us. Who did you mean by 'us'?"

"Commission people. My father mentioned people from the Commission might come by, snooping around, trying to find stuff they could use against him."

"So why'd you let me in?"

"The men my dad was talking about, the ones who silenced him, they don't ride around on bikes, stumbling around soaking wet."

"Oh?"

"No offense."

"None taken. 'Too bumbling to be evil' is the shtick I'm going for these days. You said your father was getting naive in his old age, that he did things that gave you the impression he was coming back..."

"Yeah?"

"I think he was maybe the opposite: extremely careful and mistrusting." Sam began walking to the opposite end of the garage. "You said he paid his YMCA bill every month. Did he tell you this?"

"Well no, they send the receipt in the mail, in the mail he still sends here. It's a strange thing to hold on to. They charge him fifteen bucks a month."

"I think he has his mail sent here because he doesn't want to be found. And as for the YMCA locker." Sam picked up the gym bag and set it on a pile of boxes in front of Tiana. "I think I know why he kept it, but I need your permission to check. I have a hunch."

***

*

Sam pedaled furiously back west, towards the YMCA, which he'd heard was right next to the Frank Lloyd Wright building. He wondered if he was going so fast to force himself to see this through before doubt crept in.

When he got to the YMCA, he bounded up the concrete steps and to the front desk, where a woman with cat-eye glasses stopped him. "Are you a member?"

"Oh, uh, I belong in Chicago," Sam lied, "but I don't have my card."

"We'll need you to fill out this form then."

Sam scribbled across the half-page as fast as he could before handing it back to the woman, who buzzed him in just as two teenagers walked out the door, one dribbling a basketball. Sam lunged to the side to avoid running into them. He found the men's locker room on the first floor. It was mostly empty, save a tall, slender man who looked to be in his late forties sitting on a bench near the door, putting on his gym shoes. Sam scanned the labels on the lockers, which were the color of burnt orange. Tom. Peter. The third row back on the upper right, he found it. A locker labeled "Isaac Jones."

He reached into his pocket and grabbed the small key he'd taken from Isaac's gym bag. It fit. Sam pulled off the lock and opened the door so hard it hit the locker next to it with a metallic clang. There was a manila envelope resting on the bottom—and nothing else.

Sam looked around instinctually, but the man had left, and the locker room was empty.

He picked up the envelope and sat down on a bench in front of the locker. He gently unclasped it and shook the contents onto his lap. A page fell out. "Illinois Commerce Commission, Pipeline Safety, Field Trip Report." It was from October 2 of 2001.

Sam's eyes flew over the text, snagging on words. "Inadequate corrosion protection." "No monitoring devices." "Risk of leaks." "Inadequate main replacement program."

Sam turned the envelope upside down and shook again. Another page fell out. It was an internal memo to Charlie, dated October 11, 2001. "It is my duty to protect the public interest. I can't just stand by."

Now bile was in his throat, his stomach sinking and rising—the feeling of falling. "One third of gas pipe mains. A threat to public safety that could extend beyond the purview of my study."

Isaac knew. He'd tried to warn them.

Sirens were sounding in Sam's head as he put the papers back in the envelope, placed the lock on the door, and closed it with the key. He walked out of the locker room, through the hallway, then out the door he'd just been buzzed into.

"You forgot to fill out your address," said the woman, holding up the half-sheet.

"I'm sorry, but I have to go," said Sam as he picked up his pace, the envelope shaking in his hands like a dead leaf.

Chapter 13

Sam rode west with the envelope tucked beneath his shirt, pressed against his skin. He felt for its firm surface every few blocks. The sun was slipping behind rows of houses, the taillights of cars that passed him reflecting off puddles. He realized he didn't know where he was going. A pickup truck flew by, spraying muddy water over Sam's pants. He pulled his bike over to the sidewalk and rifled through his backpack. He found his wallet, and inside it the card Greg had given him the first day they'd met.

He jumped back on his bike and rode until the burning in his thighs warmed him. By the time he reached the subdivision of identical, new houses emerging from the cornfields, he was drenched in rain and sweat. Sam pulled up to a small ranch house and lay his bike in the grass.

For a moment, when Greg opened the door, he seemed puzzled, studying Sam as if he were a strange animal.

"What's up, man? Are you okay?" Greg finally said. "Your bike—"

"It's fine. I..." Sam paused and put his hands to his face

to warm his cheeks, hoping that would make it easier to form words. "Do you have a minute?" He felt for the envelope. Still there.

"I'm sorry," Greg said, lowering his voice. "This isn't a good time. My in-laws are here." Greg quickly glanced behind him.

"Oh." Sam paused. "I'm really sorry to bother you. It's crazy of me to show up here like this." Sam turned around and headed towards his bike.

"You know what?" said Greg. Sam looked back at him. "We've got a pretty big casserole."

Sam smiled, wiping rain from his forehead. "You really don't have to."

"Sure I do, you look pathetic."

The house seemed smaller on the inside, the kitchen opening into a dining then living room lined with a carpet the color of television static. Sam stuck his open palm in the air and held it there. "Hi."

"This is my coworker, Sam," Greg said to his wife, sitting at the head of the table, her parents to either side.

"Oh, hi, I'm Ashley," she said, giving Sam a wide smile. She looked exactly like she did in the photograph, except her bangs were flat against her forehead, not held vertical with hairspray, and her large pregnant belly stretched a green thermal she clearly hadn't bought in a maternity store. "It's so nice to finally meet you."

"Thanks for letting me barge in."

"Not a problem at all."

Greg pulled a chair to the corner of the table across from Ashley, scooped a pile of casserole onto a plate, and set it down at the spot. Sam took his seat, while Greg sat at the head. The casserole was a glowing yellow speckled with beef and green peas. The rush of fat and salt from a steaming forkful put him at ease.

"So you work with this rascal?" said Ashley's father, who was sitting to Ashley's right. He spoke with a country lilt that sounded like it could be from Alabama or the North Side, face lined with the wrinkles of someone who's worked outdoors more often than not.

"Sure do." Sam smiled and looked at Greg, who grinned and rolled his eyes. "Just started."

"You've landed quite a cushy job," her father said.

Sam had to force himself not to flinch. Just hours ago he'd been at the funeral. It seems so long ago, he thought, as he took another bite, letting the mush roll around in his mouth before speaking.

"I'm still learning the ropes," Sam said.

"You're over by the Capitol, then?"

"Not too far."

"Tomorrow is not going to be fun over there." Ashley's father audibly exhaled, as if he were a doctor preparing to share bad news. "The president is coming to town."

"Oh yeah?"

"You haven't heard?" Ashley's mother had her kind smile,

147

her cheeks glittering with powder and rouge. "The police are talking about shutting down Sixth Street. They probably all want to go see him. Pastor Bill was talking about it last Sunday."

"I totally forgot," said Greg. "He's stumping for the mid-terms. That's going to be a nightmare for traffic. Sam, you're lucky you bike to work."

Sam shot Greg a close-mouthed smile as he chewed, his plate almost empty now.

"This is the one time I'm glad I don't have a job," said Ashley. "No crowds for me. They shut down Cargill's just in time." She laughed and Greg looked at her with a concerned expression that quickly vanished. "Can't you stay home with me tomorrow?" Ashley reached for Greg's hand.

Greg smiled. "I can't decide which I'd rather miss—the rally or election day."

"You're not going to vote in the midterms?" Sam asked.

"I don't know," said Greg. "Not sure it matters."

"What with the hanging chad issue they had in Florida," said Ashley's mom. "They haven't even fixed all the ballots in Illinois."

"Pretty sure it's still worth trying," Sam said tentatively. At his family dinners out East, politics was something to be debated loudly, waving pieces of food in the air and slamming the table. But here, he got the sense politics was something to dance around, a waltz he was still learning.

"I'm going to vote," said Ashley, "even if I have to drag my big belly there all by myself." Ashley patted her stomach and smiled, then left her hand there.

The room was silent. Sam wanted to ask who she was voting for but sensed this might be against the rules. "This casserole is delicious," he said, before forking the last bite into his mouth.

"Compliments to the chef," said Greg, looking at Ashley.

She shrugged. "I've got a lot of time on my hands."

Again, silence. Ashley's parents glanced at each other. Sam looked down at his plate, picked up a few stray crumbs, and put them in his mouth.

"Sam and I better go into my study," said Greg. "We have some work to discuss."

Ashley wouldn't let Sam clear his plate, so he followed Greg into the "study," a small room with a fully stocked bar, a dark grey couch facing a television with a pale grey Nintendo 64 box sticking out from beneath it. Greg sat down, but Sam stayed standing up, shifting his weight from one foot to the other.

"It seemed like I was intruding," said Sam.

"No, it was…" Greg's voice trailed off. "With Ashley out of work, everyone's worried—about her, us. It's not you."

"I'm so sorry. I know what it's like to be unemployed."

"So do I. That's what worries me."

Sam couldn't wait. Greg raised an eyebrow as Sam stuck his hand up the bottom of his shirt and pulled out the envelope, which was only a little damp around the edges. Sam carefully bent the metal clasp and pulled out the top sheet as if he were handling an ancient parchment, and held the document in the air between them.

149

"I spoke with his daughter," Sam said, looking down at Greg.

"Whose daughter?"

"Isaac Jones."

Greg's eyes grew wide. He reached for the paper as if he were about to touch something hot.

"This never saw the light of day," said Sam.

"You don't say," said Greg, a tinge of exasperation in his voice as his eyes flew across the page. He began reading out loud. "Not in compliance with federal and state pipeline safety regulations. Dangerous deterioration. Recommend a dedicated program to replace at-risk, leak-prone cast iron pipes." He stopped and looked at Sam. "Anything in his records about Springfield High?"

"He did a spot check of 210 underground pipe segments around Springfield and built his assessment from there. Springfield High's pipes weren't checked, but the Pentecostal Church of Springfield—"

"It's right across the street," Greg cut in.

"Correct. And, you guessed it, the pipes were corroded. He writes this and a week later he's applying for waiting jobs in Madison?"

"Why didn't he go public? Or sue?"

"A black man in Central Illinois calling out 'pillars of the community' like French just three weeks after 9/11? Come on. He tried to do the right thing, run it up the right channels, and they put him out to pasture." Sam handed the other paper to

Greg, who stacked it slowly on top of the page he'd been looking at, resting both on his lap.

"What are you going to do with this?" asked Greg.

"I don't know." Sam took a deep breath. "You think those pipes stop corroding at the Springfield border?" A shudder shook Sam's shoulders and moved down his back. He was suddenly aware that his suit—the only one he had—was soaked through, the threads at the bottom of his pants frayed from getting caught in the spokes of his bike. Greg's family must have been polite to not point out how ridiculous he looked, one upside to the Mid-western dancing around the obvious, he thought to himself.

Sam sat down next to Greg on a cushion that felt like it was made of velcro. "I was at the funeral today," he said, feeling a sob attempt to escape his throat. He put a fist up to his mouth and coughed into it.

Greg shook his head, seemingly more to himself than to Sam. "Do you realize what would happen if you—"

Sam's phone let out a shrill ring. A number he didn't recognize.

"Hello?"

"Sam, it's Wendy."

"Oh, hi."

"I'm so sorry to bother you." Her voice was thick with net-tles. Sam wondered if she had been crying.

"It's no bother." Sam felt his heart swell, even though he knew he shouldn't.

"I'm in a bind." She exhaled. "I hate to ask."

"Ask what?"

"Are you free tonight?"

Greg was watching expectantly—Sam realized he could hear every word of their conversation.

"When?"

"Now."

Sam looked at Greg and shrugged. "Yeah, I'm free."

"Um, okay. Random request: Is there any chance you could babysit my daughter for a couple hours? Something, an emergency, has come up and I can't explain it right now but I'm in a bind and, I need someone who I can trust who isn't a weirdo, or flakey…"

Sam's heart dropped. "You need me to babysit, your daughter? Wait—you have a daughter?"

"Five years old. The best kid in the world."

Greg leaned in, intrigued. "Babysitting? You must be high on her list."

Sam pulled away the phone with a jerk, hoping Wendy hadn't heard.

"I've tried four other—" Wendy paused. "Who was that?"

Greg shook his head at Sam, as if to say, don't tell her I'm here.

"It was no one." Sam swallowed. "I, uh, I can do it. I'd be happy to."

He hung up. Greg patted him on the back. "Man, you've got it bad. Be careful."

"Yeah." Sam reached for the paper and carefully placed it back in the envelope. Sam thought about the long bike ride, his wet shoes and socks. "I know I've asked a lot, but…" He stopped himself. "Never mind."

Greg's eyes crinkled into a smile as he pushed his wire-rimmed glasses higher on his nose. "It's not a problem. You can borrow my car," he said, reaching out a hand to pat Sam's back.

Sam had to stop himself from giving Greg a hug in return.

Chapter 14

When Wendy opened the door her eyes were lined with watercolor strokes of peach and pink, cheeks shining with tears. He saw her steel herself and when she spoke, her voice came out surprisingly sarcastic. "My knight in shining armor. Actually, in a wet and muddy suit. What happened?"

"Long story," said Sam, knowing that no matter how much he wanted to, he shouldn't tell her.

"Feel horrible for missing Raphael's funeral, Charlie sent me to the Capitol to calm down a couple hot-head legislators."

"It's fine, his brother mentioned the fund you helped raise in his speech. He was very appreciative."

"Good." Wendy turned around and led him up a stairwell to her second-floor apartment. It was downtown, not far from Sam's place, and he was already doing the mental calculation of how many minutes the bike ride would take. Wendy wiped her eyes with the sleeve of her baggy brown sweater as she gestured with her other hand. "Sorry, my place is a mess."

Framed children's drawings covered the living room wall—

colorful scribbles vaguely resembling a house, a heart, some kind of beast or animal. An L-shaped grey couch surrounded a small coffee table. Perched on her knees in front of it was a child furiously scribbling on a piece of paper. "Jessica, honey, come say hi to Sam." The girl looked up—she had brown-black eyes and cinnamon hair whose chin-length cut made her head the shape of a mushroom.

"Hi, Sam," she said in a high-pitched voice, then looked down at her page and resumed her drawing, biting her bottom lip in concentration.

"Sam is going to be watching you tonight while I'm gone." Wendy seemed to be trying to make her voice as soothing as possible for her daughter.

"Okay." Jessica didn't look up this time.

Wendy walked into the kitchen and Sam followed. The fridge was covered in drawings and school pictures held up with magnets. An opened box of Cheerios was on the table. Wendy looked at home here, a mother raising a young child. Alone? Sam wondered. It had to be alone.

"I can't thank you enough," she said, her voice trembling. "I don't know exactly how long it will be." She paused and peered into the other room at her daughter before speaking. "I have to post bond for a friend, and they close at nine."

"I'm sorry," said Sam, remembering the jail he'd been sent to after he sat in the street in Seattle and police sprayed tear gas from a large canister straight at his face. He'd tried to pull his baseball cap over his eyes and press his chin to his chest, but it hadn't helped. They didn't let him wash the chemicals from his body the entire twenty hours he was in jail.

Sam looked at her and said, in what he hoped was a reassuring voice, "You should get going."

"Thanks again. I can't tell you how much you are helping me." Wendy looked at Sam for a moment then walked into the living room and through the door, shutting it behind her.

Sam walked up to the table and crouched next to Jessica. "What are you drawing?"

She didn't say anything, just put down her green crayon and reached for a purple one, then pushed it purposefully across the paper in the shape of an arch.

"Is that a rainbow?" No answer. "An umbrella? A giant nose?"

At that, Jessica giggled. "It's a unicorn tail."

"Where's the rest of him?"

"I haven't drawn the body yet. Can you do the eyes and nose?" Jessica handed Sam a crayon, and he slowly etched out a snout, nostrils, eyes.

"What color should the horn be?" he asked.

"All of them. Here, let me help." Jessica took on the tone of an expert patiently helping a novice.

As Jessica drew squiggly lines in a shape vaguely resembling a horn, Sam held still, worried that if he moved wrong this moment would somehow pass. He hadn't spent much time with children, although he thought he might want some one day, if he could ever achieve financial solvency. He thought about the documents he'd left in the glove compartment of Greg's car, the financial ruin they'd rain down on him if he had the courage to do the right thing.

"Will you help me color in the legs?" Jessica handed him a pink crayon, which he dutifully moved in small, zigzag motions until the legs, which looked more like heavy cement blocks, were a soft raspberry.

"Here, let me finish it. You're nicer than the other babysitter. He's also a grownup boy." Jessica pressed a purple crayon hard into the paper then moved it rapidly, her head moving in the opposite direction.

"The other babysitter—he's also a grownup boy?" Sam tried to make his voice as gentle as possible. Am I grilling a child over her mother's love life? Sam thought to himself. No, just friendly banter.

"My mommy's friend." She held up the piece of paper to Sam and said, "It's done." The picture looked more like a horse that had gotten caught in a tornado, but Sam pressed his hands together into applause. "Bravo! Bravo!" he said, stopping himself from asking if it was the guy with the good hair he saw Wendy with from the other night.

Jessica smiled, showing two rows of tiny teeth. "Can you hang it on the bulletin board?"

Jessica grabbed Sam's hand and pulled him into the kitchen. On the wall to the left was a small corkboard, three pins each holding piles of drawings beneath them. Sam reached for the pin in the middle with his right hand, with his left hand pressing the pile of papers against the corkboard to keep them from falling. But just then, Jessica pulled hard on Sam's left hand. "Can I have juice?" she said.

The papers fell and scattered across the kitchen floor. "Sure, just one sec, let me clean this up."

Sam kneeled down on the tiles and used both hands to sweep the papers into a pile, each one covered in colorful squiggles, swirls, and straight lines. His eyes stopped on a piece of paper that was different from the rest: It was almost blank, save a single line of adult handwriting, small and neat, at the center of the page.

Charlie: 3994 Sunnyside Avenue.

Sam dropped the page and remained frozen on his knees as it drifted to the floor.

"What are you looking at?" said Jessica, crouched in front of him, staring at the piece of paper.

"Nothing, nothing." Sam rapidly picked it up and pushed it to the bottom of the pile then pinned the stack back on the bulletin, the picture of the unicorn on top facing outward.

He opened the fridge. "What kind of juice do you want? I see orange and apple."

As he reached in to grab the carton of orange juice, he flipped open his phone and quickly typed the address into a text message to himself, the door blocking Jessica from seeing. A beeping sound a second later told him it had gone through. I am not spying, he told himself, this is an act of self-defense. With the information I've got, I can't be too careful. Still, the rest of the night, Sam felt like a thief, and when Jessica asked him to play hide and seek, he did it as though his gusto were an apology, practically shouting when he found a child beneath the obvious lump of blankets and clothes on the couch. "No way! I can't believe it," he said, as Jessica broke out in gleeful laughter before yelling, "Again! Again!"

When she grew tired of hide and seek, it was time to tell a story, finishing each other's sentences with what came next. The tale meandered from a lost dog to a princess to a dangerous wolf, each plot twist making seemingly less sense. Yet Jessica remained utterly committed to the game, so much so that he didn't dare try to end it until she finally asked him to read her a book. He reached for "Goodnight Moon," the same book his mother had read him as a child, thinking this was a kind of fun that was pure tedium—yet somehow more delightful because of it. When Jessica started to nod off, he lay a thin blanket over her, then leaned back and closed his eyes until the chaos of the day turned into soft echoes. He didn't wake up until Wendy was standing over him, a faint smile on her face.

"Oh, hi, sorry, I must have fallen asleep."

"Nothing to apologize for." She reached down to Sam's left and pulled the blanket higher on Jessica, who made a burrowing motion with her head, but didn't wake.

"Is your friend here?" Sam sat up and groggily looked around.

"He doesn't get out for another two to four hours. They like to dump people onto the street in the middle of the night."

"Will you need me then?"

"No, he can take it from there. I got him out, after that—" A black plume of anger rose from her words. She stopped, collected herself and started walking to the kitchen. Sam followed, feeling light on his feet, his head still syrupy with sleep. They stood in front of the bulletin board for a beat. Sam pointed at the drawing, "Her masterpiece. I mean, ours."

Wendy looked at Sam with a sad smile, then jerked her head away and studied the drawing, as if she were a buyer at an art gallery.

Sam prodded, "Your friend, is he…"

"The man I was with the other night? Yes."

"Oh? He didn't strike me as the 'getting arrested' type."

"He did strike the pole he hit as one I'm sure. DUI, his fourth in two years." Wendy took a deep breath, looking away from the drawing but not quite at Sam. "That crowd, his friends, the guys who work at the Capitol, they can't name a DOE parking lot without getting trashed. Usually some State Senator makes a phone call if someone gets pulled over, or they recognize the expensive suits and haircuts and know who juices this town, but I guess this time Milton—"

"His name's Milton?"

"I guess this time Milton had the bad luck of being pulled over by some Boy Scout."

"They're a dying breed."

"Who, honest people in Illinois government?"

"People named Milton. But yeah, that too. Seriously though, was he born in 1924?"

Wendy let out a faint laugh. "It's always on his terms. He doesn't need to see me until it's eight p.m. and he's been arrested, again. And then all of a sudden he's serious. But not when it's time to pick Jessica up from soccer. No, he's always too busy, staying late at the Capitol."

She stopped herself and looked at Sam. He leaned in. "Why do you stay with him?"

"Saying I'm 'with him' would be putting it strongly," Wendy

said. "To be honest, I don't have a good answer. Things just…" Wendy paused again, staring long and hard at Jessica's drawing before finishing her sentence, "happen."

Wendy pitched forward and pinched the bridge of her nose, looking down as her face turned red. Sam saw a tear roll off of her chin.

Wendy wiped her face with the back of her hand, still staring at the floor. "But look at me, talking about commitment with a guy who's spooked by keychains."

Sam chuckled softly to tell her he wasn't offended, that the joke had landed.

He reached over as if by reflex, taking each of her hands in his. She pivoted towards him and looked up, with her face so raw it seemed warm water would sting it.

He meant to just kiss her cheek, but when she leaned in, her lips found his. They were warm and salty, and the kiss, if that's what it was, lasted for only a moment before Sam pulled back, now wide awake, and dropped her hands. They fell by her side.

"I'm sorry," Sam mumbled. He felt something inside him ache as he looked at the unicorn picture on the bulletin board, remembering what was underneath, what he had taken.

"Don't be," Wendy said softly, not moving back an inch, looking at him. "You have nothing to apologize for."

Sam walked through the living room and paused at the door. "She's a great kid," he said, looking at Wendy. "A total blast."

Wendy smiled. "She is, isn't she? Thanks."

"It was really my pleasure." With that he was out the door,

racing down the stairway, and walking out into the chilly night, not quite wintry yet, but almost.

The ride home was a blur. Sam thought he could still taste the salt of her lips as he drove slowly home, down a cobblestone street, past a small outdoor playground, softly illuminated by the moon. The thought of it made his heart scrape in his chest like a trapped animal. She had kissed him—or had she? He replayed the scene, trying to remember the order of events. When he reached for her hands, had she reached back? Did she turn her face towards him or away? If this was all part of a ruse, Sam didn't care. The train was already in motion, its engines thudding and whirring.

Sam pulled up to his apartment and reached for the glove compartment. The envelope was still there. He grabbed it and walked towards the front door, eager to collapse into his bed, even though he doubted sleep would come.

Just then, Gertrude walked out on the front porch. "Sam! Sam! Vhere have you been?"

Sam sighed. "Hi Gertrude. It's been a long day. How are you?"

"Fine, fine. You come in so late. Are you seeing a girl?"

"That's private."

"Ah, I see. Your friend vas here."

"My friend?" Sam did the math in his head. Anyone remotely resembling a friend was already accounted for.

"Who was it?"

"Not a man of many vords."

Sam's heart was pounding. "What did he look like?"

"He vas a little younger zhan you. His uniform had a bird on it, an eagle, but not like German of arms, more spread out."

Sam stood frozen on the bottom stair, remembering Daryl, the security guard from the water tower wearing the eagle insignia. I don't think I'm being paranoid, he told himself. Who else could it be?

When he lay down and tried to sleep—the blankets pulled up to his ears, envelope tucked beneath his mattress, a chair propped against the lockless door to his apartment—he wondered, what did Daryl want with me?

Chapter 15

In the morning, Greg asked Sam over text to drive his car
to work, saying, "I don't want to wade through that morass."
Sam had woken up early enough that he missed the worst of the
traffic, although four blocks from work he had to wait patiently
while a police officer wearing a yellow vest waved each car, one
by one, down a right-lane-only street.

He found a parking spot two long blocks away and, the envelope with Isaac Jones' report tucked under his jacket on his right
side, began the walk as the sun peeked in behind the mid-rises
at a low angle. He could still feel the events of yesterday on him
like a thin film, but his head was aching and heavy. Just focus on
keeping the envelope safe, he told himself. You can figure out
what to do later.

Half a block away, he stopped. There were about fifteen
people clustered in front of the steps to the Commission, one
person in a wheelchair. It looked like some of them were holding signs. Could this possibly be overflow from the Bush rally,
he wondered? No, the crowd wasn't white enough, the signs
too homemade. Sam walked closer until he could make out the
words, handwritten in sharpie, on a white poster board. "Release
the safety reports." Another: "What are you hiding?"

"Hey hey, ho ho! The public has a right to know," chanted the crowd, surprisingly loud despite its small size. Sam realized half of them were wearing the red shirts emblazoned with One Springfield that he'd seen at the meeting. Four people were wearing purple "Justice for Janitors" shirts.

Sam squinted then walked quickly to the person in the wheelchair. "Mrs. Belinda, remember me? I met you the other day at the meeting." She was wearing a red One Springfield shirt, eyes dusted with bronze shadow.

He held out his hand, but Mrs. Belinda didn't shake it. Instead she looked up at him and, in a flat tone, said, "Yeah, I remember you. Sam Golden."

Sam extended his hand a few more moments before putting it in his pocket. "What are you doing out here?"

"What does it look like I'm doing?"

The look on her face told Sam he'd had his chance, now she was done talking to him. Still, he pressed on. "You going to be out here all day, or—"

Mrs. Belinda cut him off. "Come back and talk to me when you have something to say. I'm not here for your thumb twiddling."

Sam took a step back, stung.

He could hear the crowd chanting behind him as he walked up the stairs and into the building. No one on his floor was at work yet but, still, Sam shut the door to his office. He sat at his desk and pulled out the envelope, staring at its burnt yellow exterior before slipping it into his desk drawer and shutting it. But after a few seconds he pulled it back out and tucked it under his shirt, against the bare skin of his right side. This envelope would come with him everywhere. He couldn't take any risks.

The sun was higher in the sky now, filling the room with milky light. Sam sat with his head in his hands before opening the box of testimony, now at his feet. It was his job, after all, to testify, and that was still what he planned to do. The company, of course, had been unresponsive to his follow-up questions, and it wasn't like his bosses were going to come to his defense. But omissions contain information too, Sam thought to himself.

He'd always worked best when he was fueled by anger, pounding out independent media center articles about the police stopping him for jaywalking on the way to a protest, or writing a student union statement against the greed of the administration. However inexperienced, once he started writing, he became a captain steering a ship, even within the perpetually couched language of testimony.

The company has deviated in a number of ways from the allocation methodology approved by the Commission in its most recent gas cases without providing a meaningful explanation why.

Sam hunched forward while he typed, his back making the shape of a C, unaware that he was clenching his jaw until a knock on the door jolted him. It was Angelo, reaching for his trash.

"Hard at work?" he asked.

"Yeah," said Sam.

"Lots of protesters outside."

"Sure are."

"My union's out there."

"Oh, right. SEIU. I should have put two and two together."

"I'm shop steward for the building, even though there aren't many of us."

"But at least you have a union. That's gotta help, right?"

Angelo gave Sam a serious expression. "Did it help Raphael Sanchez?"

Sam said nothing.

Angelo continued, "We're going to get a better contract next time. None of this two-tiered business. We just have to figure out how."

"When does your current one expire?"

"December."

"Well, let me know how I can help."

Angelo paused in the doorway. "Okay, I will."

He left the door open. Moments later—it could have been one minute or five—Sam looked up and saw Julie standing in the doorframe.

"Meeting in the conference room in five minutes. It's office-wide." He still hadn't earned back his "blessed morning," let alone eye contact.

Sam looked at the lines of text on his computer screen, still unsure of where he'd steer it.

When Sam walked into the conference room it was already full—Keith, Greg, the triple J's and a few people from inspections around the table, Charlie at the head, and Wendy in back, outside the circle, sitting in a chair against the wall. Sam took a deep breath and walked around the table to take the chair next to her. When she looked at him, there was no hint of a smile. Sam just nodded his head, and then turned toward the front of the room, his heart beating against the manila envelope he'd tucked under his shirt for safekeeping.

Just then, Phil walked in and sat in a chair to Charlie's left, his hair a pomaded silk, beard shaved down to a calculated stubble. When Sam caught his eye, Phil nodded once and then smiled warmly, as if to say, why do you look so startled? I belong here. Like Mrs. Belinda before, Sam offered no response, moving his gaze to the wall behind Phil.

"Alright, let's get started," Charlie said in a humorless voice. "As I'm sure you're all aware, this is a sensitive time for the Commission. For those of you who actually got to work on time, you had to walk through a protest to enter the front door. We worked with the police department to clear the party, but this probably is not the last of it."

Keith cut in, "Have you seen the letter to the editor from the Citizens' Utility Board? And the stuff SEIU, the janitors' union, is saying about wanting to see the reports? We haven't even eliminated terrorism yet, and they're going on about releasing the safety reports."

"May I remind you that 'we' are not confirming or eliminating anything," Charlie said, venom in his voice. "That is entirely up to the police department and the FBI, who are working diligently with our partners at United to solve the case." Charlie gestured towards Phil with an open palm.

Sam glanced at Wendy. Her hands were pressed tightly together, as if in prayer, and she was leaning forward, body angling towards Charlie. She always seemed so deferential when she was in a room with him, Sam thought, as though she were hanging on his every word. Why? With a sudden jolt, Sam remembered the paper and the mysterious address. Charlie's? What had it meant?

Charlie's voice was louder now, a jet engine revving into motion. "I'm getting it from all sides. The Citizens' Utility Board is breathing down my neck, a bunch of whiny liberals are protesting outside, and law enforcement is telling me they need time to conduct a confidential investigation because public safety is at stake. And now I have the governor calling me saying we have to tell the public something."

The room was as silent as an empty house. Sam sat perfectly still, worried that the slightest movement would make a crinkling sound.

"Our game needs to be tight." Charlie was yelling now. "No, flawless. A single word from any of you to the media could mess this up for all of us. We don't need any explosions. Anyone wants to talk to you, send them to me or Phil. I don't care if it's *The New York Times* or a high school newspaper. You keep your mouth shut."

Why would we go to Phil? thought Sam, his face growing hot. He's not even part of the Commission.

Phil leaned back in his chair and crossed his leg, his right ankle resting on his left knee, as if he were sitting with friends around a campfire. "I know you all must be feeling a lot of things," he said in an intimate voice. "Believe me, it's been an intense time for all of us. United is collaborating closely with law enforcement and the FBI, treating this investigation with the utmost urgency and integrity. We know how important it is to the community and everyone in our extended networks."

What was an 'extended network,' and was Raphael Sanchez in it? Sam looked over at Greg, who was staring at his notebook, brows scrunched so tightly they formed a tiny grid between his eyes. Maybe I was wrong to tell him, Sam thought. He must feel as scared as I do.

"At a time when so many possibilities are still on the table," Phil continued, "and nothing—including terrorism—has been ruled out, we can't let public speculation get out of control. It's impossible to overstate the extent to which that would undercut our priority of protecting public wellness and safety."

The rest of the meeting felt like a public interrogation. Charlie went one by one to each of the departments, asking for a recap of how they were responding to the public perception crisis. There was nothing for anyone to share, other than reassurances that they weren't talking to the press. Keith spoke with such conviction about the importance of letting the law enforcement investigation run its course that Sam wondered whether it was possible he didn't know about the bad reports. If he didn't know, maybe almost everyone else didn't either. Except for Charlie and Phil. Who else would have run Isaac out of town?

Suddenly the whole room was looking at Sam.

"I'm sorry, I missed what you said."

Charlie reiterated, "Anything to report?"

"No, no, nothing." Sam looked down at his hands, certain his neck was crimson. When he looked up, Charlie was looking at Wendy. She was holding his eye contact, saying nothing. And then, as if a spell had been broken, Charlie dismissed the room with, "Alright, that's all," and then walked out the door.

Sam stood up and, eyes at his feet, shuffled towards the door. He had to stop himself from dodging when Phil reached out his right hand, exposing a pale green prayer bead, and gave Sam a hearty pat on the back. Sam kept his arm pressed tight to his side to keep the paper from falling to the ground.

Just as he exited the room, he heard Charlie's voice behind him. "Sam, wait a second."

Finally, someone in the office who wanted to talk to him—and his boss, no less.

The two stood outside of the room near the door, waiting for the last person to file out. When the hallway was clear, Charlie leaned towards Sam with a faint smile, the venom drained from his voice. "Hey bud, good news. We're sending you to some critical infrastructure security classes in Carbondale."

"I'm sorry, what?"

"These classes have gotten rave reviews. Should be good for you."

"Oh, well, I'm in the middle of the United case and would really like to stay focused on that."

"That's exactly why we're sending you. We see this as an investment in your professional development. Believe me, it will help your career in the long run. This is a field you need to know these days. Especially with the United case."

Despite his cheery tone, Charlie seemed to Sam like a lion about to pounce. Sam resolved to say as little as possible.

"When do they start?"

"Tomorrow morning. There's a bus that leaves today at four. We already bought you a ticket. We'll let you take the rest of the day off to pack your things."

Sam looked at him and straightened his shoulders. Then in a voice that he hoped betrayed nothing but calm, said, "Thank you for the opportunity. I better head home now to pack my things."

But as he said it, Sam felt a hard knot tighten in his chest. Why are they sending me, he wondered. Are they trying to get rid of me?

Chapter 16

When he ran into Greg's office, face flushed, Greg, as expected, agreed to meet Sam at the diner across from the Greyhound station. Sam hoped the walk home to pack his bags, and then to the restaurant, would help clear his head. But it only filled his lungs with cold air and exhaust fumes as he trekked the perfectly flat blocks.

At the diner, Sam was met with a handmade "Springfield Strong" sign taped to the glass door, which opened to a floor and walls the color of coffee stains. Sam sat at a table next to the window, facing the muted television in the corner, backpack at his feet. He ordered pancakes, just like he and brother used to eat when they were kids, back when, as his mother was fond of saying, Sam had been "husky."

Just as Sam forked a bite of pancake into his mouth, Greg walked through the door. When he sat down, Sam offered him a menu, but Greg put up a hand. "Nah, I'm not hungry." Sam put down his fork and knife and leaned towards Greg.

"I think they're trying to get rid of me."

Greg raised one eyebrow, his chin resting on his hands.

173

"Charlie just told me I have to go to Carbondale for critical infrastructure security classes, whatever that is."

"He told you this just now?"

Sam nodded.

Greg drummed his fingers on the table and looked at Sam, saying nothing.

"If they want me out of the picture, why don't they just fire me?" asked Sam.

"You think they would fire the rate analyst for the United case right now? I'll give you two seconds to imagine how the optics of that would play out. The publicity around this case is your best protection right now."

Behind Greg's head, someone had turned on Bush's speech from the Illinois Police Armory, just a few blocks away from the Capitol, catching him mid-sentence. "And that's why I went to the United States Congress and asked them to join me in the creation of a new department of homeland security, so we can better coordinate all the activities that are taking place at the federal level," he said in his thin, nasally voice. The camera showed a close-up of his face, his frown forming the shape of the letter M, eyebrows like caterpillars crawling towards the center of his forehead.

When Sam turned back, Greg was staring at him. "You know what I would do if I were you?"

It was Sam's turn to be silent.

"I'd get on that bus, take those classes, come back and say, 'Thanks for sending me. I learned a lot.' And then I'd keep my head down for a while and pray that when this all blows over I'll still have a job."

Sam stared back. He imagined another reality without United's corruption; no exploding gas line, no grieving family. He thought Greg and he could have been good friends. His mother always told him that you loathe that in people which you most dislike in yourself, and admire most those traits you lack. That, he realized, is why he liked Greg so much: he was curious without being superior, caring without being self-loathing. In him, Sam saw the normalcy he craved after years of jumbling about. But he knew this reality, where they watched Illinois football games on weekends and "Uncle Sammy" came over for beers, wasn't the one they occupied any longer. He had already said—and seen—too much. Sam leaned in. "I found an address, this strange address written on a piece of paper at Wendy's house that said 'Charlie: 3994 Sunnyside Avenue.'"

"That could mean anything. You're getting a little loopy, Sam."

Sam lifted his shoulders to his ears then dropped them limp at his side, as if to say, so what?

"In my previous life, when I worked fighting real estate developers from kicking poor people out of their homes, I got good at researching this kind of thing," said Sam. "Phil liked to call me 'scrappy,' now I think he might have been insulting me."

Sam lowered his voice to a harsh whisper, not exactly sure why. "I've been mulling the right moment to duck out to go to the County Clerk's office to follow this lead. Charlie—"

"You don't know it's a 'lead,' Sam. You don't know anything. It could be the address of Charlie's dry cleaner."

"It's not a public-facing business, that's the first thing I checked online. But to find the owner I have to go look at the physical records."

"Sam."

"What?"

"You're starting to sound like a crazy person. Just get on the bus." Greg sighed. "The property will be here when you get back, all these 'leads' will."

"Yeah, maybe you're right."

"You don't make it easy to be your friend." There was an exasperation in his voice that Sam hadn't heard before.

"We're friends?"

"Well, we'll see how this goes." Greg laughed then stopped abruptly. "Seriously, I'm going to pretend I didn't know about those documents or the fact you snooped around Wendy's apartment. I suggest you do too."

The screen buzzed behind Greg's head. "The reason I brought up the threat from Iraq is because I understand the new realities. I see the world the way it is. Saddam Hussein is a threat to America. He's a threat to our friends. He's a man who said he wouldn't have weapons of mass destruction, yet he has them."

Sam thought about the first day they met, how Greg had seemed like a scared, skittish animal. Now, Greg was asking permission to flee.

I will let him, Sam resolved. I won't drag him into this any further.

"I'm sorry to be short," said Greg, rubbing his thinning hair into his forehead. "Ashley's on bed rest."

"Oh god, I'm so sorry. What's wrong?"

"She had started to go into preterm labor, but they were able to stop it. Should be okay." Greg sighed. "We're all pretty stressed. I'm trying to hold things together."

"Well if we're officially friends now, I'm a shitty one. I've been so focused on myself. Is there anything I can do?"

"Just don't get your ass fired and run out of town." Greg's laughter sounded like a rattling engine.

***

The Greyhound station was the same colorless blue as every other, a large, glass door opening to the buzz of televisions and a smell that immediately reminded Sam of the feeling of riding a bus for two days without ever stepping outside or changing your clothes. He'd done it to get to Fort Benning, Georgia for a protest against the School of the Americas. After that, he'd sworn to Phil that he never would again. Phil had laughed at him and said, "Greyhound is jail on wheels."

Sam walked to the counter and handed his license to a woman who could have been either twenty-five or forty-five. She printed him a ticket and pointed him to gate 16 in the left corner of the room farthest from the door he'd walked in. He sat on the black padding of a chair connected by cold metal to a row of seats in front of the gate, facing a television. A man was sitting three seats down, cowboy boots protruding from worn jeans, a handlebar mustache that swallowed up his bottom jaw.

The screen briefly flashed an image of the chief of police and the governor, a recap from the press conference, the volume too low for Sam to hear. "Getting the hell out of this town?" asked the man a few seats down.

Sam gave a single nod to the man, who smiled then looked back at the screen, which had moved on to an image of construction for a new car detailing business. Sam's gaze wandered to the front door. The sun streaming through it forced him into a long blink.

When he opened his eyes he saw a man walking through, back-lit. He was tall and thin, in a black shirt and baggy jeans, hair shorn close enough to his head that Sam could see the outline of his skull. He could either be a soldier or a tweaker.

The man walked toward the ticket desk. He had a boyish face and a strong jaw. Sam's heart turned to icicles. It was Daryl from Eagle Security.

He's come for me, was the only thought in Sam's head.

Before the newscast could move on to a new scene, Sam had grabbed his bag and run towards gate 16. Not daring to look back to see if he was being chased, he pressed the door. It was open.

Hands shaking, Sam pulled out his bus ticket and handed it to the driver, a squat man with white hair, who was standing outside the door. "This is my bus," Sam panted.

"We don't board for another five minutes."

Sam reached into his pocket and handed the driver a wad of bills that he didn't bother to count. "I need to get on now."

The driver looked around then snatched the money. Sam bounded past him up the stairs.

When he sat in his window seat, he let his body fall to the left, feet in front of him, so that he couldn't be seen outside the window. He lay perfectly still, feeling his pulse race in his temples, wondering if Daryl had seen him.

People started boarding the bus. He sat up straight in his chair and leaned his face against the seat, covering it with his hands. He peeked at some of the people getting on. The man with the handlebar mustache. A woman holding a baby.

He buried his eyes in his palms, thinking it somehow made him safer if he couldn't see what was happening. Or maybe I'm just a coward, he thought.

Someone walked to his row and stopped. Sam thought he could sense a person hovering, faintly make out their quiet breath. But he couldn't bring himself to look.

"Sam Golden?" The voice sounded stern. When Sam looked up, Daryl was towering over him, backpack on his shoulders, hands balled into fists. Sam pressed himself against the window.

"Why'd you run away from me?" Daryl softly growled.

"I, I wasn't running." Sam was surprised at how thin and high-pitched his voice sounded, like a scared child.

"You don't remember me, Sammy?" He swung the bag off his shoulders and tossed it below the seat next to Sam. "I met you at the water sanitation plant. This is my seat. I'm going with you to the security class. They wanted to train up a few people."

"Oh." The word escaped Sam's mouth in a weak gust. "Of course. I remember you."

"I went to your house last night to talk to you about the trip, but your landlady said you weren't home." He sat down.

"That was you?" Something inside of Sam loosened. Maybe he wasn't out to get him. "Why didn't you call?"

"I was in the neighborhood and figured I'd just drop by."

A voice came on the intercom. "Alright folks, this is the express bus to Carbondale, Illinois."

Sam studied Daryl, who seemed even younger up-close. "How did you get my address?"

"Phil. He and Charlie and I talked and we agreed one of your points of professional development is that you lack an appreciation of security and safety in this line of work. Part of our private-public cooperation is making sure everyone's on the same page in that regard, from tough guys with eagle badges on their chest to skinny number-crunchers who listen to opera." He smiled almost hungrily. "You know?"

Sam tried to swallow but it felt like his mouth was filled with sawdust. How did he know I listen to opera? No way Sergeant Bench Press was that observant. He must have tossed his place looking for the Jones file.

Sam tried to stifle a rising note of hysteria in his throat. The idea of Daryl searching among his things, and for what, suddenly gave him the sensation he was tumbling—like he had looked down and realized there was no floor. Daryl had let it slip, or perhaps he wanted him to know.

The bus started moving slowly in a backwards U out of the parking lot. Sam figured he had seconds before the driver moved the car into drive and set its passengers on an unstoppable course south.

Before he knew what he was doing, Sam reached between his feet, grabbed his bag, and leapt over Daryl's long legs into the aisle. When he reached the bus driver, Sam pleaded, "I need to get off this bus."

"Boy, you can't make up your mind."

"I'm going to be sick. Let me off."

Sam looked back and saw Daryl walking down the aisle towards him.

Sam lunged his body against the door, just as the driver opened it, and fell onto the pavement on his side, still gripping his bag. In a "Fuck you," the driver tore away with a screech. Sam stumbled to his feet and, this time, looked back.

As the bus turned right onto a side street, Sam could see Daryl's silhouette through the window. He appeared to be haggling with the driver, but the bus didn't slow down.

Sam reached into his pocket to look at the time, pulling out two flip-phones: his and Daryl's. He seemed to have snatched Daryl's Nokia as he rushed out. It wasn't an accident, he told himself, it was instinct. With no way to make calls and two hours to the next stop, Sam had a head start on Daryl and whoever the hell was trying to get rid of him.

He turned around and ran towards downtown.

Chapter 17

Sam's footsteps thudded against the pavement. As he gulped in cold streams of air, his vision focused on the bare tips of branches lining South Grand Street. What have I done? was the question ringing through his head.

But he knew what he'd done. He'd chosen—crossed over some invisible line. In one simple act, the drab office, the steady paycheck, had been tossed off a precipice. He was falling with it, his stomach turning with exhilaration and dread.

Sam wasn't sure if it was impulsiveness or idealism driving him. But as his breathing grew more labored, the distinction began to blur. A cold wind sent a tear down his cheek. He wiped it away with the sleeve of his coat, never slowing his pace.

***

By the time he got to the County Clerk's office, Sam was damp and steaming in the brisk air. The office was an ancient stone building, roofline sprinkled with statues and ornamentation.

He climbed a long set of stairs up to the entrance, and then to the second floor, where a tall, white-haired man with tortoise-shell glasses stood behind a desk.

"I'm looking for information about a property." Sam wrote down the address he had seen on Wendy's refrigerator—3994 Sunnyside Avenue—on a small white piece of scrap paper, hoping the clerk couldn't see his hands shaking.

"You don't have a date?"

"This is all I've got."

"We'll see what we can do."

The clerk disappeared into the back and returned moments later with two big books. One was for residential transactions, the other for businesses. Sam watched as he thumbed through the first for what seemed like five minutes.

"I don't see anything that meets your criteria. Let me check the commercial transactions." The clerk opened the other book, the pages crinkling in the silence.

Sam heard high, rhythmic beeping coming from his pocket, like a bird chirping. He flipped open Daryl's phone and looked at the glowing green screen. An incoming call from Ray Moore. Where have I heard that name? Sam wracked his brain. He thought of Charlie, the snotty frat boy beside him, tall with shiny hair brushed away from his forehead. The InfraGard liaison.

For a moment, Sam almost wondered what Moore was doing calling some low-level security guard—and then realized. It was no coincidence that Daryl was supposed to be sitting next to him on a bus headed downstate. Sam was on the radar of some important people. And what would they do when their call went unanswered?

Sam snapped the phone shut so hard the clerk looked up at him before returning to the book. As the clerk rifled through the pages, Sam tried to take deep breaths, but the exhale kept catching on his throat.

"You haven't digitized your records yet?"

"Not starting until next month." The clerk didn't look up.

"Chicago digitized two years ago."

"Good for Chicago."

The clerk continued shuffling through the pages.

"Bingo, I think I've got it."

The man turned the book around so both could see. "The commercial property was sold by 35 Cards Capital LLC for $1.2 million. The sale went through, let me see, December 20, 2000."

35 Cards? Sam wondered. What could that possibly mean? There are 52 cards in a deck, he couldn't forget that. His mother loved to accuse him of putting one up his sleeve during the endless gin rummy games that somehow never got dull on his visits out East. He thought of his mother's slow shuffle, the way she lifted the cards into an arch then sent them clattering down, Jokers, Queens, and Kings crashing into each other. Still nothing.

What about a Pinochle deck? That had 48, a number he knew from that summer in middle school he'd become obsessed with playing it while his brother grew tanned outside, getting scrapes in the ravine and playing kickball in the field next to the local UConn campus.

Sam looked up at three County Clerk employees behind the

desk milling about. "Sorry to bother you all, but, uh, does anyone know what deck has 35 cards?"

Blank silence. "Anyone?" Sam was speaking with an urgency that didn't match the tone of the otherwise silent room. He briefly wondered if they thought he was losing his mind. Sam recalled reading once that a lack of sleep can begin to mimic symptoms of schizophrenia. When was the last time he slept?

He calmed his voice. "Sorry to bother you. I'm just trying to figure something out. What game has 35 cards?"

A woman with short auburn hair in the back-left corner perked up. "Baseball," she said, chewing on her gum. "But that's 40."

"I'm sorry?"

"The St. Louis Cardinals, they're called the 'Cards,' and they have 40 players on a roster, not 35. Around here everyone just calls them the Cards. Maybe that's what they mean."

"Right, of course. Does anyone know who wears 35 for them?"

The woman looked on. "Hold on one sec." She looked over her shoulder and yelled out, "Dan!"

An older balding man with glasses peaked his head out. "Yeah?"

"35 on the Cards, is that Edmonds?" She was chewing her gum even louder.

"No, Morris."

Sam remembered the first day he'd met Charlie—the framed

picture of Matt Morris throwing a pitch. It could be a coincidence, but not likely.

"Can you tell me when 35 Cards Capital bought the property and how much he paid?" Sam asked.

"It's right below. They purchased it five years earlier for a price of $47,500. These guys made quite a killing. Relatives of yours?"

"Acquaintances. How might you explain such a big jump in the sale price for a business property like this?"

The shrill beeping resumed in Sam's pocket. Someone was getting worried about Daryl.

"Do you want to answer that?" the clerk asked.

"No, no, I'm going to let it go to voicemail."

The two said nothing as they waited for an end to the beeping. Sam wondered whether the bus had stopped at a rest area by now, how long he had before Daryl reached a payphone. Or maybe someone on the bus had a cell phone Daryl could borrow.

When the beeping stopped, the clerk's face pinched into a grimace of concentration. "A lot of things can change for a property over five years," he said. "A neighborhood can suddenly become desirable. Traffic patterns can change and bring more people to the area. If cars start flowing down a street, then everyone wants to do business there. Or a major retailer may move in and lift the fortunes of a neighborhood."

"Do you have the buyer's name?"

The clerk pressed his long forefinger to the page. "It's right there. The Healthy Futures Alliance."

This was the same Healthy Futures Alliance that gave Thomas French a platform for handing a giant check to an "underprivileged" teenager. The same Healthy Futures Alliance United used to justify its rate increases.

If it was what it looked like, and the Healthy Futures Alliance was used to pay off Charlie, Wendy had known. And odds were, given what Sam already knew about her role in stonewalling Allison, Wendy was not planning to use this information for good. He didn't want it to, but he knew everything added up to Wendy somehow being in on it, or at least complicit. The realization was a hard pebble in Sam's gut.

"Mind if I make a copy of this page?"

"I'll do it for you." The clerk disappeared into the back, then returned a moment later and handed Sam a warm piece of paper. Sam slipped it into the manila envelope, alongside the other documents, then walked outside and sat on the steps. He reached into his pocket and picked up a phone, this time his own. He hadn't wanted to call her until he was sure, but certainty was almost in view, and he was out of time.

"Sam?" Allison seemed surprised.

"I need you to meet me at the Clerk's office. Now."

Allison was silent for a beat. "What's going on?"

"I can explain when you're here. Bring your car. And call any contacts you have at the Illinois Secretary of State's office and find out who the principal is for 35 Cards Capital."

"35 Cards Capital LLC?"

"Yes."

"Are you going to explain any of this?"

"I will when you get here." He flipped his phone closed.

Sam pulled out Daryl's phone and pressed the unlock key, but the screen told him he needed an access code. Sam put the phone in the front pocket of his bag, suddenly glad that he had packed clothes. He wasn't sure where he would stay, but home wasn't safe when they knew where he lived.

Allison pulled up in a blue Ford Fiesta, and Sam ran down the stairs and jumped into the passenger side.

Allison looked at him. "I wasn't gonna come, I don't usually like taking orders from sources but—"

"You found out who owns 35 Cards Capital?"

"Yes. And obviously I'm intrigued. Tell me what's going on here and what this has to do with Charlie Harper."

"Do you know how to get to 3994 Sunnyside?"

"Sam?"

"We need to go now." Sam looked at her. "Trust me."

As Allison drove north, Sam recounted the last two days, which felt like months. She sat up straight, both hands gripping the wheel, as Sam heard himself say, "I think they're after me." He soldiered on, explaining how Eagle Security had searched his house, and adding that he thought Healthy Futures was a front group. When Sam got to the safety reports sitting in his bag, she didn't move to look, instead keeping her eyes plastered on him, as though if she looked away for a second he might do something rash.

"Whoa, whoa, slow down, Sam," Allison said. "I know you've been through a lot, but let's take it down to a six and you pick up again at the part with the address. You found it at the home of Charlie's assistant?"

"Wendy, yes."

"Should I ask why you were in her house?"

"I was babysitting her kid, it's a long story—" he gasped, eager to get it out. "The point is, I can't think of a benign reason why she would have this address, especially since she's the one who buried the Jones report that warned the gas pipes were faulty."

"She's Charlie's hatchetman?"

"It's the most logical explanation. I found out that employee ID was hers." Sam squinted at the dim street sign. "Take a left up here."

The two saw small houses, gas stations, and then mobile homes jutting from brown lawns. "Strange place to put a $1.2 million property," Sam said.

"Yeah, no shit," Allison said, slowing the car as she turned right onto Sunnyside. The street was lined with small ranch houses, similar to Greg's subdivision except a quarter of them were boarded up, porches as sunken as soggy bread. Allison began surveying the space. "I grew up in a mobile home near here."

"You did?"

"Bonafide trailer trash, and I'm telling you, there's no way a house sold for that much in 1995. The rich kids didn't get on the bus until at least a mile-and-half that way where the Oak Meadow subdivision is."

"You sure?"

"The way they treat you, you don't forget a thing like that. I could draw you a property value map using the scars on my knuckles as a reference."

Sam looked at her as she stared ahead, putting the car into park. "So that's why you do what you do?"

Alison looked ahead. "We're not there yet, pal." She darted out of the car as Sam let out a faint chuckle.

They had stopped in front of number 3994. It was clearly abandoned. Its grey paint was peeling, half the windows were boarded up, and tall weeds billowed in the wind. There was a "For Sale" sign outside.

"I can't believe this is even worth the $47,500 Charlie paid eight years ago," Sam said.

They got out of the car and started walking toward the property, a camera slung around Allison's shoulders. Sam dialed the number on the "for sale" sign, and the woman who answered told Sam to hold on when he inquired about the property for sale at 3994 Sunnyside Avenue.

A minute later a man got on the line. "What do you want to know about the property?"

"Is it still for sale?"

"Sure, sure."

"How much is it?"

"You can have it for $40,000. How much do you want to pay? This is a highly motivated seller. Just make me an offer."

"Let me talk to my wife and get back to you."

"Okay. Remember, the seller is eager to make a deal."

Sam hung up the phone and looked over at Allison, who was standing on the lawn taking pictures of the house. "Healthy Futures Alliance bought it from Charlie for $1.2 million and now they want to sell it for $40,000?" he said.

Allison put the camera down and turned to Sam, a breeze blowing her hair away from her face.

"You know what this means," said Sam.

"Healthy Futures is bribing the Commission."

"Yes but—" Sam stopped himself.

"Yeah?"

"I don't get it. Assuming this is what it seems like it is, what about oversight? What about the inspector general, the FBI?" Sam's inner skeptic was taking over. He needed to make sure he wasn't throwing away his career on a paranoid misunderstanding.

Allison clinched the keys, looking up at Sam. "I get it, these things sometimes have benign explanations. But this," she paused, looking up at the balding roof. "This is a hard one to explain."

Sam nodded.

"Two Illinois governors have gone to federal prison, Sam. It's more than possible they were busy reeling in bigger fish. In any event, we should get going, we have work to do." She walked quickly towards the car, but after six feet she stopped, realizing Sam wasn't following.

"What is it?"

Sam looked up dazed. "Wendy has to be in on it. I didn't want to believe it before, but that's where I got the address from. And I know she's the person who told you to get lost when you inquired about the safety reports."

"You mentioned that. Look, I know this hurts right now, but we'll have to mend hearts later. "

"Of course."

"You have much bigger problems, Sam. Look—"

"I know."

"No, I need to say this, we need to be clear," said Allison. "You know that under the first amendment I'm more or less protected for publishing these safety reports. But you, as a source—"

"I know."

"Let me say it out loud. I need verbal confirmation that you understand what you're getting yourself into. These are stolen government documents. The FBI is probably investigating this, under the specter of terrorism, no less. Given the atmosphere, you could be facing ten, twenty years in prison."

"Atmosphere?"

"Say you understand, Sam."

Before he could respond, Sam heard his phone ringing in his pocket. He looked at the name on the caller ID. Wendy. Why is she calling me? he thought. She must know I'm not on that bus. They're trying to find me. Before he knew what he was doing, Sam flipped open the phone and pressed talk. He wasn't sure whether it was curiosity, or the desire to hear her voice—still, despite everything.

"Sam, hey." Her voice was halting.

Sam stood in silence. He looked over at Allison and mouthed "I understand."

"Sam, you there?"

"Hi, Wendy, how are you?"

"Oh, I'm fine. You on the bus?"

"Yeah."

"How's it going?"

"Greyhound is a heavenly way to travel."

Wendy laughed. "Okay, well, I was just calling to say hi, and…" She stopped herself.

"Yes?"

"Thanks for your help last night. It would be nice to, um, do that again under better circumstances."

Sam looked over at Allison. She was a foot away from the

porch, camera angled at a boarded-up window. "Yeah, I'd like that."

"How much longer until you get to Carbondale?"

"Oh, a couple of hours."

"What's that in the background? It sounds like wind."

"Oh that—this is a pretty noisy bus." Sam cupped his hand around the receiver. "Look, I'm low on battery juice. I should go."

"Oh." Wendy sounded stricken. "Well, okay, let me know when you're back and if you want to hang out."

"I will."

Sam hung up the phone and buttoned his jacket until it was tight around his neck. Before Wendy mentioned it, he hadn't noticed how windy it was. Now it felt like the wind was tearing through him. Or maybe it was nerves. Either way, he was trembling.

Chapter 18

"Where exactly are we going?" Sam asked. They were in Allison's car, its floor covered in a thin layer of old newspapers and notebooks, a few empty Diet Coke bottles rocking against Sam's ankles in the passenger seat. They were rolling down Sunnyside, away from Charlie's house.

"Well, Daryl could be in Carbondale by now, so we can't go to your place, because they know where you live. And we probably shouldn't go to mine." She pressed the gas as they turned right onto a busier street, a pickup truck coming fast behind them. "We're going to go to my mom's. She's pretty off-the-grid, and she's right up the road. Once we're there, we can figure out what to do." Allison sounded like she was deciding on these steps as she said them, and Sam just nodded.

About two minutes later they turned left onto a wide street covered in brown leaves, both sides lined with white and pastel mobile homes, stacked almost as close as bricks on a wall. Allison slowed down and nodded at two men drinking out of Natural Light cans, leaning on a Ford Mustang, by far the most expensive thing on the lot. It was parked in front of a sky-blue trailer.

"Y'all still drinking that mop water?" Allison shouted out of the window of the car, which had rolled to a stop.

One of the men in plaid with a scar over his eyebrow fired back, "Yeah, you still drinking Busch beer?" He let out a self-satisfied chuckle, turned to his buddy. "Get it? She likes bush."

"Yeah, I'm gay, that's fucking gold. You used that joke on me two years ago, get fresher material."

Chase turned back to his friend who nodded and confirmed, "It's true, you did."

"We'll catch you guys on the way back," Allison told them. "My coworker and I are in a bit of hurry."

"You got it, always more Natty Lights to go around, Al."

As she hit the gas, Sam leaned in quietly. "What's their deal?"

"Those dorks? They're harmless. Gearheads mostly. Chase worked at Cargill's 'til it closed. Now I don't know what the hell he's doing." Allison stopped her car four homes down, in front of a beige trailer with brown shutters, hoisted on cinder blocks.

"Yeah," Sam said, still sitting in the car. "Seems like a lot of people lost their jobs there. Sad, really."

"Look, we don't have a lot of time." Allison opened her door but didn't get out of her seat. "I promise we'll get to your ethnographic study of Springfield's white trash some other time."

"I'm not gawking, you know. I was born working class. It's just, I was a socialist for eight years and it's hard to turn off."

"Yeah? What happened?"

"Burned out, I guess."

"Relatable. I was curious."

"About what?"

"Why a small-town, middle-tier analyst was so self-righteous about utility rates. I didn't have ex-Marxist shit-stirrer on my Bingo card, but it makes sense."

"Is that—"

"Sam."

"Yes?"

"We gotta table this."

"Right."

"Shadowy conspiracy of corporate and paramilitary interests is chasing us, remember?"

"Of course."

Allison's mother opened the door to her mobile home and stood at the entrance, wearing an oversized black t-shirt and bleach-blue jeans, her blonde hair cropped close to her head. She watched with her arms crossed and a smirk on her face as Sam and Allison walked up.

"Oh, hello?" Allison's mother looked over at Sam with barely veiled confusion.

Allison saw her face, then looked back at Sam. "Relax mom, he's just a source."

"It's so good to see you, sweetie." Allison's mother grabbed her and pulled her close.

"Just a source?" Sam said half-kidding.

"What are you lobbying for here exactly—'friend'? I've known you a week."

"Acquaintance?"

"When you come out as gay, if you're not very specific, people begin to speculate."

"Fair enough." Sam held out his hand to Allison's mother. "Hi, I'm Sam, Allison's source."

"My name's Denise, it's a pleasure."

"He's helping me with that United story I told you about, Mom. We need to hang out here for a bit."

"No problem, honey. Y'all come on in."

Allison walked past her mom inside, and Sam followed behind her. The interior had a crimson carpet that cut off at the kitchen on the left, which was floored with shiny brown tiles. Allison sat down on a small couch on the other side of the home, the back of her head to a large window that gave a view of Allison's car, parked on the curb of the street they'd just driven down. The walls must be thin, he thought, a piece of cake for someone like Daryl to break through.

"You okay, Sam?" Allison asked.

"Yeah, why?"

"You had a weird expression on your face."

"Oh sorry, I was just tired. It's not every day I outrun a mercenary."

"Yeah, well that's probably a good thing. If you were going to do that more often, I'd suggest getting in better shape."

Sam looked down at his thin wrists and laughed. "I like that wall hanging," he said, pointing at the large purple weaving on the wall to his right. "Who made that?"

"She did. She loves doing macramé." Allison, who seemed to be reluctantly indulging Sam's small talk, gestured to her mother, who was in the kitchen washing dishes, her back to them. Allison pulled out her cloud-grey Libretto laptop and propped it on her knees. A tinny symphonic sound told them the computer was on.

"Just one sec, let me get the dial-up working."

Denise walked to the couch with a wire. "Need this?"

"Mom, you were listening?"

"How could I not?" She walked back into the kitchen, which was fully in view yet somehow seemed like a separate room, sectioned off by the cabinets that ringed its walls. Allison shook her head as she plugged the wire into the side of the computer.

"What are you doing?" Sam asked.

The computer started making shrill phone dialing sounds, followed by a series of beeps and screeches.

"I'm going to show you something. I think you've earned it." Allison angled the computer towards Sam, and he hunched towards it, elbows resting on his thighs. "I got this the day of the explosion."

"You've been holding out on me?"

"I told you, I wanted to see if you were serious, which now I obviously know you are. Look," she pointed at the screen.

The email was from anonymous64925@hotmail.com, with the subject line, "Tip." Sam read it out loud. "Dear Allison, I know about the story you are writing. I'm someone with inside knowledge and would like to keep my identity anonymous."

Sam looked at Allison. "You had a leaker?"

She gave him one nod.

Sam kept reading. "This may be nothing, but after the explosion I decided to go into the Commission's server, which I never use, and see if I could find the safety reports. When I logged in using my ID and password, I got a pop-up window telling me my access has been revoked since January 2001. I never log in, so I didn't realize until then. Like I said, it might be nothing, but I found it strange."

Sam reached into his bag and pulled out the copy the clerk had given him. "The sale went through in December 2000—a few weeks before."

"Yeah."

"So, just weeks after Charlie gets $1.2 million from United by way of the Healthy Futures Alliance, this guy, whoever he is, loses his access to the safety reports. Jesus Christ." Sam ran his fingers through his curls. "Do we have a smoking gun yet? Isn't that a term you guys use?

"That's what cops say—in the movies. And, I don't know if the gun is smoking. But it's warm."

"Warm? What more do you need?" Sam leaned back into the mushy couch cushions behind him. "I bet this is my friend Greg, or at least I'm pretty sure. Who else could it be? Everyone else at my office is crooked or a boy scout for the company or spying on me." Sam realized he was talking rapidly. He exhaled then said, "Did he say anything else?"

"I asked him to find me on AOL instant messenger. He messaged me once to see if his tip had turned up anything."

Sam heard the unmistakable ding of an AOL instant message, two tones tumbling into each other.

"Oh that's weird," Allison said. "He's messaging me right now." Allison angled the computer away from Sam. "I can't type while people are watching."

"He's asking me if I'm with you," she said.

"Wait, what?" said Sam. "How would he know?"

Allison's hands flew over the keyboard as dings came in rapid succession.

"What's he saying?" asked Sam. Allison didn't respond. She was stopped, her fingers suspended over the keyboard, mouth half open.

"What is it?" Sam pressed. "Tell me."

"They know where we are. Daryl's phone has a tracking device." For the first time, Sam heard Allison's voice shake. "They're coming for us."

"Who?"

"I don't know. We need to leave now."

"Are you sure?"

"That's what he says. You want to take a chance?"

Allison looked down at the computer and started typing. "Shit." It came out loud enough to fill the home.

"What?" asked Sam. "What?" he said again when she didn't respond.

"The internet cut out."

Allison's mother, her back to Sam and Allison, was talking on a land-line phone connected to the wall in the kitchen. Denise barked into the phone, "Chase, don't ask questions. I need you over here now with your Mustang."

"Mom, what are you doing?" Her voice came out in a frantic screech. "You have no idea how bad your timing is."

Her mother turned around. "No shit, honey. I can hear everything."

"Mom?" Allison's voice was softer now.

"I'll take care of this. You pack up your bags." There was a matter-of-fact flatness in Denise's voice.

Sam wasn't going to wait. He picked up Allison's computer from her lap and put it in her backpack. Just as he zipped it up, he heard two honks of a horn and whipped his head around. The man in flannel with a scar over his eyebrow had moved his Mustang in front of Denise's place. Sam noticed the boxy red car had giant scratches down the side, as though a tiger had dragged it with its claws. Sam turned around to Allison's mother.

"That's that guy, Chase?"

"He lives down the street," Denise replied. "I've bailed that boy out so many times, he owes me one. And maybe he can finally put his drag racing skills to use." Allison's mother extended her hand to Sam. "Give me the phone."

"Which phone?"

"Which one do you think? The one with the tracking device." Sam plunged his hand into his pocket and put Daryl's phone in her hands.

Allison's mother ran outside, her arms swinging wide on either side of her. Allison and Sam followed behind her. "Chase, I want you to ride as far and fast as you can out into the cornfields and when you see someone tailing you—"

Sam cut in from the doorway. "Probably a big black Suburban."

Denise nodded. "When you see someone in the rearview, you drop this out the window and turn right around and come home, just as fast."

Up close, Sam saw Chase had red lips that opened into a big smile. "Anything for the mother of my future bride."

"Shut up, Chase, it's never going to happen," Allison said, the color returning to her face.

"Who's that?" Sam asked, pointing to a black car that had turned down the road to Allison's mother's home, about a quarter of a mile to their left.

"Go now, Chase. And don't let that son of a bitch catch you.

Treat this like a race, okay? Do everything you have to do."
Denise sounded like a drill sergeant. Chase shrugged, peeled
backwards, screeched into drive, and flew in the direction of the
black car.

Denise turned to Allison. "You go too. Get in your car the
opposite way."

"Mom, what will you do?"

"Don't talk back to me. Go. Now." Her voice had steel in it.
The black car was about 300 yards away, maybe 200.

"Love you, mom," Allison said, and then ran to her car.

Sam was about to follow her, but felt a firm hand grip his
shoulder. "Take this." Denise thrust something into his hand. It
was cold and heavy enough to move his hand down half a foot.
Sam knew what it was before he looked. Still, the sight of the
small, black gun made his spine prickle.

"I don't want this."

"Take it." Denise did not sound like she was in the mood for
negotiation.

"I don't even know how to use it."

"Allison does."

Sam put the gun in the front pocket of his backpack, his
hands shaking as he closed the zipper.

Allison slammed the gas before Sam could shut his door. He
pulled it closed against the wind and looked back at Denise, who
was standing in the doorframe of her home. She was holding
something small and black in her hands. Sam shivered. Another

gun.

In the side mirror, Sam saw Chase flying towards the black car like cargo on a zipline. It seemed, for a moment, the two cars would collide. But they didn't: Chase swerved and shot right past.

Sam watched as the black car slammed its brakes in the middle of the street about a hundred yards from Denise's house, sending leaves twisting into the air. It made a three-point turn and took off in the direction of the Mustang. Sam watched as the black car grew smaller, until Allison took a sharp right.

Sam reached down and fumbled through the bag at his feet. The manila envelope was still there. Not that it could have crawled away. But still, he thought to himself, we haven't lost yet.

Chapter 19

It wasn't difficult to convince Allison to drive to Greg's. As she gripped the steering wheel, her knuckles considerably whiter than on the ride there, she acknowledged she didn't know where else to go and, if Sam trusted Greg, that was enough. But maybe, Sam thought, she didn't want to drag any more of her people into this. When they parked in front of Greg's house and stepped out onto his lawn, Sam felt a prickle of doubt. "I told him I wouldn't get him more involved, yet here I am," he said quietly. Allison said nothing.

When Greg opened the door, a look of shock, or maybe it was annoyance, flashed across his face.

"Greg, I'm so sorry to show up here," said Sam. "Believe me when I say I didn't know who else I could turn to."

Greg was studying Allison, who was standing to Sam's left. "To what do I owe the pleasure?"

"I, uh, I," she stammered.

"This is the journalist, Allison."

Greg stared, saying nothing.

"Was it you?" Sam spoke softly to Greg, like he was trying not to scare away an animal. "Did you warn us?"

"You're anonymous64925?" Allison's voice came out in a squeak.

Greg unfastened his gaze. "I'm sorry?" he mumbled.

"You were the person who told us to run," Allison said, a little louder this time.

Greg coughed into his hand. "Oh yes, it's me. I'm sorry. It took me a moment to register..." his voice trailed off.

Sam tossed his arms around Greg and pulled him in towards his chest in a hug. Greg flung forward, and Sam was surprised by how thin he was beneath his loose pale-green button-up shirt. "Thank you," Sam said in his ear, tears burning the corners of his eyes. Sam let go, stepping back a foot, as Greg stood in the doorway, leaning against the frame with his left arm.

"If I knew you were going to come here, I might've reconsidered." Greg had a sardonic, if a bit shaky, smile on his face.

Sam crossed his arms and shook his head good-naturedly. "All that time you were telling me not to rock the boat."

"Don't look so self-satisfied. I never follow my own advice."

"You never passed along my information to Allison."

"Not mine to tell."

Sam smiled. "How did you know?"

"Know what?" asked Greg.

Allison took a step forward and brushed away a strand of golden-brown hair from her forehead. "Look, we can do all of these friendship forensics later. Right now, we need to go inside and write this article. Our best hope of protection is getting this thing out in the world and naming and shaming them, so that when they try to ship us off to a black site or whatever it is they plan to do with us, people are watching."

"Of course, of course." Greg turned around and walked toward the dining room table, Allison and Sam following behind. With his back to them, Greg said, "Let's try to keep our voices down. My wife Ashley is on bed rest. She's sleeping."

"Shit, Greg, I'm sorry." Sam spoke quietly as he walked around the table and sat facing the window on the far wall, an instinct telling him to sit where he could see if anyone was coming. "You're never going to believe what we just went through, like something out of a Steve McQueen movie."

"Let's not oversell it, Sam." Allison sat down to Sam's left, pulling her computer out of her bag. "Charlie and his Eagle Security goons, or whoever they were, tried chasing us down. But we lost them."

"Really? Oh wow." Greg seemed more confused than worried.

Allison nodded yes as she put a notepad, covered in notes, on the table. "If we were worried the story was a dud, I think when your story's subject tries to stalk you at your mom's house, it's a pretty good indication there's something there."

"I knew it," said Greg. "I knew there was. It's why I helped, you know, pass along information. But I never—"

"Knew the whole puzzle?" Sam excitedly jumped in.

"Yeah."

"We more or less have the pieces put together, just a few more blank spots," Allison said, and for the first time all night, she let out a smile.

"I just have to call my in-laws." Greg pulled out his cell phone. "They were going to come over tonight to bring us some food. Excuse me." He turned around and walked through the living room, then out the door, shutting it softly behind him.

When Sam put his bag on the table, it made a loud thump. He pulled out the manila envelope first, delicately emptying its contents and placing them on the table—the pipeline safety field trip report, the internal memo. He gave the envelope a tiny shake, and a small piece of torn paper landed face up on the table. The employee ID number that Allison had scribbled down, that Sam had later discovered belonged to Wendy. He forgot he'd put it there.

Sam picked it up, folded it into a small triangle, and put it in his pocket. However she may have wronged me, he thought, remembering Jessica asleep on the couch, we don't have to make Wendy part of the story.

"Allison, don't freak out. Your mom gave me this." Sam reached into the front pocket and slowly pulled out the gun, facing it towards the far wall, then set it down on the table directly in front of him.

"Jesus, Sam."

"What was I supposed to do, leave it in the car?"

"Why would she give you this? And why would you take it?"

"You ever try saying no to your mother?"

Sam heard the front door close. When he turned around, Greg was ten feet behind him, staring at the gun.

"Greg, I'm sorry. Allison's mom gave it to me when the Eagle guys were tracking us. It felt safer on the table."

Greg was pitched forward, his hands balled into fists, lips yellow around the edges.

"Be careful with that." Greg's voice was low and calm.

"I will," said Sam. "Why are you talking like you're trying to negotiate the release of hostages?"

Sam laughed, but Greg didn't. Greg silently walked to the table and sat to Sam's right, closer to the gun.

Everyone was staring at it, a small, angular chunk of black metal, its frame ribbed like the gills of a fish. Sam noticed how quiet the house was, something you never got in Chicago, where the outdoors always comes clattering inside. Allison let out a long sigh and, in his periphery, Sam saw her put her forehead in her hands. "I need to make sure my mom and Chase are okay. My phone is in the car. I'll be right back."

When she stood up and walked out the front door, Sam leaned back in his chair and put his hands behind his head, his elbows fanning out like wings. "Do you think the triple J's will miss me?" Sam looked over at Greg, hoping he'd hear the good nature back in his friend's voice.

Greg let out a chuckle, and Sam felt a wave of relief. "Of course they will. You give them so much to talk about. When you're gone, they'll have to go back to discussing whose milk is expiring in the fridge, and which high school football team is going to win district."

"I'd rather be talking about those things. Boring sounds pretty nice right about now. But you know who *I* will miss?"

"Who?"

"The Triple J's and their disturbingly precise breakdown of middle school football," said Sam.

Greg let out a laugh. "Can't talk about high school without knowing who the next batch of recruits are."

Sam reached over and gave Greg a pat on the back, holding his hand there. "I'm running with the A team now." He pointed at the window, where he could see Allison sitting on the hood of her car, talking on the phone. "I know I'm not always the best judge of character." Sam reflexively pressed his hand against his right pocket, where Wendy's employee ID number was. "But you can trust Allison. I'm sure of that."

"Okay." Greg looked over at him, with the same intelligent, skittish expression he'd had when he first walked into Sam's office and introduced himself. "Just, now that you're here and safe, I need you to think. Don't do anything crazy." Greg made a motion with his hand as though he were shooting a basket.

Sam shook his head and smiled. "Too late for that. But for the first time in a while, I believe in what I'm doing. So there's that." Sam shrugged.

Greg shook his head.

"I could really use a beer right now," said Sam.

"We have plenty in the kitchen. Mind grabbing me one?"

Greg pointed at an open doorway to his left.

Sam walked through and found the large, white refrigerator pressed up against the wall separating the kitchen from the dining room. He went to open the door, but then stopped, his hand resting on the handle. Along with a photo of Ashley's parents and a job posting for a salon receptionist, a magnet was holding up a small off-track betting ticket: 8274.

Wow, he'd really hung it on his fridge. Maybe we're closer friends than I realized, Sam thought to himself, a wide grin on his face as he remembered Greg's rule about always betting the last four of his social.

But when he read the ticket again, his smile dropped. Something was wrong. He'd heard those numbers before.

Sam let go of the handle and stepped back from the fridge. Fingers shaking, he reached into his right pocket. He unfolded the torn piece of paper and looked down at Wendy's ID number. Written in pencil was, "323768274."

What an idiot I am, he thought. That's a social security number. At the Commerce Commission, your employee ID *is* your social.

Sam put the paper back in his pocket and felt his knees go soft. He caught himself with his arm against the fridge, sending the magnet crashing to the ground.

It had been Greg who told Sam to watch out for Wendy, and it had been him who confirmed her employee ID number.

"Everything okay in there?" Greg shouted from the other room.

"Yeah, just knocked a magnet off the fridge." Sam's voice

came out threadbare.

Sam looked at the door that probably opened to the garage, and wondered if he should run. But then he thought about the papers on Greg's dining room table. That was his entire story.

He picked up the magnet and papers on the floor and put them back on the fridge, then reached inside and grabbed two bottles of beer. He fumbled through the drawers until he found one with a bottle opener. Next to it was a small knife in a blade guard. Willing his hands to stop shaking, he picked up the knife and put it in his right pocket next to the piece of torn paper.

As he walked towards the doorway carrying a cold beer in each hand, he felt a burst of hope. He thought of Wendy's wavy hair, her lithe arms, the way her eyes changed from vulnerable to derisive in an instant. He hated that, in this moment, Wendy's affection was the first thing on his mind—but he'd pegged her wrong, and he couldn't be happier.

Sam stopped in the doorway and felt his breath escape him all at once. Greg had moved into Sam's seat. He was directly in front of the gun, his right hand resting on the grip.

The only thing for Sam to do was move forward. He sat in the chair to Greg's left, where Allison had been, and put Greg's beer on the table, beside the gun. He pressed his own to his lips, the bitter taste giving him a jolt of energy. Maybe, he thought, when Allison comes back inside, I can signal to her. Or her arrival will be distraction enough to grab the gun. He flitted his eyes at the window to see if her call was wrapping up.

She wasn't there. The car was empty.

Sam breathed in and out. He looked at Greg, whose eyes were following his, then turned his gaze to a cocoa-colored stain on the table.

Sam exhaled audibly, thinking that if he just played this cool, Greg wouldn't know that he knew, and he could buy time. For what, exactly, he wasn't sure. But once he could get the thudding sound of his own pulse to die down, perhaps he could think of something.

It was Greg who spoke first. "I was thinking about what you said at the OTB."

"Oh yeah?" Sam spoke slowly. Did this mean Greg knew I saw the betting card? he wondered to himself.

Greg was motionless, his face sapped of all emotion, while he spoke. "Here's what I don't understand. You think regulators are captured by utilities—so compromised that you have to work outside of the Commerce Commission to gather evidence, expose the system. So why have regulators at all? What makes you different from a libertarian who wants to scrap all oversight and let companies operate unencumbered? If you were a communist or whatever, wouldn't you want to protect regulators, who already have a bad enough rap?"

Sam looked at Greg's hand, which was still resting on the gun, then back at him. He could feel his panic rising like a gas in his lungs. It's all so unfair, and they're going to win, he thought. The papers were still scattered on the table, Allison's computer wide open, but Sam didn't dare reach for them. And he didn't dare ask why she hadn't returned.

"You have me all wrong," said Sam. "It's not just that regulators are captured by a single industry or company. It's about the class interests of government and its institutions, even the institutions meant to protect the most vulnerable. Everything bends towards the capitalist class."

"That sounds like *Lord of the Flies*. You see yourself as

an idealist, but you don't sound like one. I don't see any good guys." Greg's voice turned melancholy—a low, discordant note.

Sam felt the slow boil of defiance. "There are plenty of good guys. This old lady at One Springfield had to huddle around her stove when she couldn't pay her heating bill, and now protests outside of our office, dragging herself there in her wheelchair. The only thing regulators can do is tilt the scales towards people like her, right?"

"Oh, so regulation is a tool for class war?" Greg said, and for a moment, Sam thought he sounded genuinely curious.

Sam leaned forward in his seat as he pressed both palms into the table, the proximity to Greg's hand on the gun raising the hairs on his forearms. "There already is a class war. It was class warfare when the Commission let United Gas raise the rates again and again. And it was class warfare when Charlie helped United sweep a public safety crisis under the rug. There are no pure regulatory institutions under capitalism—libertarians are right about that, but they're wrong about why, and what to do about it."

"You see, there are picket lines everywhere." As Sam said this, he picked up his right hand, pressed his index finger into the table, and dragged it in a straight line, as if to mimic a picket line, inching closer to the gun before stopping. "At the Commerce Commission, with every information request, every testimony filed, you're either taking a small step towards correcting a staggering power imbalance, or you're reinforcing it. You can go about living your life as though the wellbeing of eight million people isn't in your hands, convince yourself you're just a technocrat, a paper pusher. But that won't bring Raphael Sanchez back. That won't pay for an elderly widow's heating bill. That won't—"

Sam stopped. A sleepy voice had come from the kitchen

doorway. Both Sam and Greg whipped their heads in its direction. "Greg?" Ashley was standing in a white nightgown, her large belly tenting the sheer fabric, arms and legs thinner than the last time Sam saw her. Ashley's wheat-colored hair was tied in a low ponytail, loose strands stuck to her forehead. She opened her eyes wide. "Oh my god, Greg, what is that gun doing there?"

"Ashley, go back to bed." Greg spoke with a force Sam hadn't heard before, startling him up out of his seat. On his feet, Sam flung each arm across the table, gripping the safety report and internal memo in his left hand. When he bounded towards the front door, he stumbled, but caught himself in a sprint, arms swinging like a rag doll's.

Ashley let out a thin scream, or yell, but it sounded far away. Sam reached for the door knob with his right palm, clasping the internal documents in his other hand. He was almost outside, not that he knew what he was going to do when he got there, but at least there would be a wall between him and Greg.

The metal was cool on his hand, and the knob turned easily. Too easily. The door flung towards him like a sail catching a wind. Sam tried to run through but couldn't move.

Someone was blocking the doorway. He was a little taller than Sam, wiry arms surprisingly solid. Sam looked at his face. Daryl.

"No—" The word caught in Sam's throat.

Daryl's hands were on Sam's shoulders. Sam wasn't sure if he was lifted or shoved, but the next thing he knew he was against the wall, flapping his arms like a butterfly pinned to a mount, still clutching the papers. Daryl held him in place. Sam thought he could feel all ten of Daryl's fingers press into his shoulder blade.

"What do you think you're doing?" Sam shouted.

"We have reason to believe you are in possession of classified documents," said Daryl, his voice matter of fact, eyes straight ahead. "I'm authorized to detain you until the appropriate authorities can be contacted."

No one moved. Sam could smell what he guessed was Lysol wafting from the kitchen. Or was that Windex? Sam noticed a photo on the opposite wall. Greg and Ashley on their wedding day. They looked like teenagers. He thought he could still see the baby fat in her smiling round cheeks.

Sam saw another figure step through the doorway and towards him. A hand reached over to straighten Sam's collar, its wrist wreathed in pale green prayer beads. Phil. Sam jerked his head away and Phil withdrew his hand. "Whoa there buddy, rough day?"

Sam dropped his arms to his side, still gripping the papers, and looked over at Greg. The gun was dangling awkwardly from Greg's left hand, like a broken limb. Sucking in his lips, eyes wide, Greg gingerly met Sam's gaze.

"These the in-laws you called?" said Sam.

"I was trying to help you." Greg's expression was pleading, but he made no motion to help Sam. "I like you. You're my friend. But I have a family to take care of. You think this is how I want to spend my time?"

"You gave me Isaac Jones' name."

"You think I ever would have done that if I thought you'd find his daughter? I knew he was long gone. I never tried to set you up, Sam. I protected you as long as I could."

"So, our 'friendship.' That was so you could spy on me? Manage me?"

"No, it was real, I swear." Greg stopped mid-sentence. "Look, I was told to keep an eye on you when you started. I keep an eye on all internal United-related matters. But then you went off like a paranoid nutcase, accusing people—"

"'United-related matters?' Funny. I thought you worked for the state."

"Ashley's been out of work two years, Sam. Around Christmas time, when Charlie stuffs our stockings with a personal bonus, what are we supposed to say?"

"Greg, that's enough," Phil jumped in, his voice stern.

"Charlie wanted to get the FBI involved much sooner," Greg continued, unphased. "But I talked them out of it. I told them I could calm you down. I tried protecting you."

"The FBI is involved? I'm guessing it's not to investigate United for murder." Sam shot a look at Phil.

"Greg, what's happening?" Ashley was in the doorway, hand covering her mouth, as if to stifle her own scream.

"Ashley, please go back to bed. I'll explain all of this later." Greg put the gun on the table and stepped towards her, but she took a step away, and the distance between them remained the same.

"The FBI?" Sam insisted again. "What the hell does the FBI—"

"You think you can just run around with confidential documents related to critical infrastructure, handing them to private citizens, using unsecure channels?" Phil wadded a tight fist in front of his own mouth, beads jangling, and lowered his voice. "You don't think this poses a major risk to national security? The FBI is going to prosecute, Sam, make no mistake. It was us who kept them at bay."

Now Phil moved his hands into a prayer sign and brought them to the center of his chest. "I'm telling you this from a place of respect."

"I don't work for you," Sam shouted. In his periphery he saw Ashley, still in the kitchen doorway, take another step back. "God, what happened to you?"

"I told you," Phil replied, "I do public-private partnerships. I interface with the public and private world. You're a public employee causing undue conflict for the private side, my employer. Thus my presence here." Phil paused. "What I want to know is what happened to *you*, Sam." He had the tone of someone politely informing a waiter his steak was overcooked. "It's easy to criticize, to lash out, but what are you building?"

Sam looked at Greg, who cast his gaze to the floor, then back at Phil. Despite everything, he felt a swelling in his chest. "You, with your prayer beads and your $2,000 suits," said Sam, breathing heavily, spitting as he spoke. "I see you."

Sam wanted to say that he wasn't alone, that the bravest things he'd done had been with others. But Sam learned long ago you're not allowed to incriminate anyone but yourself. He paused and looked at Phil. "I'd forgotten, but you reminded me."

Phil lashed out, "Forgotten what?"

Sam grinned. He was calm for the first time in days.

"This is why I thought you'd be perfect for this role," said

Phil. "You think you're an idealist, but it's your streak of nihilism we were after. Granted, I'd rather you hadn't gone off on your own and tried to be a hero. But it's all working out in the end."

Sam looked over at Greg. "This role? What's he talking about?" Greg's face looked perplexed. He said nothing.

Phil moved towards Sam. "You ever wonder why the person who negotiated the last United case only lasted three months?"

Sam couldn't respond.

"You should always read your employment contract carefully. Erstwhile labor activists like you should know that." Phil's voice was dripping with mock disappointment. "You're subject to a probationary period. Six months. If you're fired before that, it doesn't trigger an investigation. And since you, and the dupe before you, signed off on all the paperwork—"

"Paperwork? I didn't sign any paperwork. What are you talking about?"

"When you're desperate, you're careless," said Phil. "You're a smart guy—brilliant, in fact—but your lack of interest in detail is pathological."

Sam's heart fluttered as he thought back to his first day, the bitter relief that he'd landed a job—any job—and his eagerness to please. "Just sign here, here, and here," Charlie had said. Sam had responded with a flick of a pen and a wide smile.

"But those were standard—"

"Those were you signing off on the Commission's assessment that United Gas' safety reports are—how do your people like to say it—kosher. And that was you saying you sign off on everything. You own this now. I see you, Sam, no one but you."

220

Phil laughed. "You think a company like ours wouldn't have an insurance policy—ten insurance policies? You're just one of them, Sam. But don't worry, once the media attention dies down, you'll be gone, back bussing tables for tourists at Planet Hollywood Chicago or whatever rat hole we pulled you out of."

Phil made a sweeping motion with his right hand, palm facing Sam. "I'm thinking, headlines read, 'Illinois Commerce Commission Fires Analyst with History of Insubordination, Vows Internal Investigation.'"

Sam looked at Greg, who was slowly shaking his head. "I didn't know, Sam, I really didn't. This is above my pay grade."

Words bubbled in Sam's head. "I'll find a way to expose you." It sounded corny to him, but what else was there? He blurted, "I know you turned your back on us because you felt you had no choice. But I'm struggling to understand at what point you went from keeping your head above water to true believer."

Phil let out a sigh and dropped his hands to his side. It seemed his magnanimity was beginning to wear. "Sam, I honestly didn't think any of this would happen to you. I thought I could throw you some money and you'd pivot to the private sector like everyone else, especially given how desperate you were. But, well, a pipe malfunctioned, you started making wild accusations, and here we are. But honestly all this 'why'd you do it?' recapping is boring me—I'm going to hand this off."

He was right, Sam thought, words were pointless now. But then he remembered. "Where's Allison?" No one answered. "Where is she?"

Steps sounded in the front door, and everyone turned to look at once, Daryl never loosening his grip. A pro, Sam thought to himself with a sneer.

But then the sneer turned to something else. He remembered being unemployed in the ninety-five-degree heat, plastered to his leather couch. The feeling that things would never get better—that each whiff of hope was a delusion.

Because Wendy was standing there—her jaw firm, eyes un-smiling. She wasn't looking at him, but at Phil. In the cadence of a cop on a power trip, she said, "Charlie sent me. Just in case you need help. He called right after you left."

Whatever spark Sam had seen in her before was gone—she was stone-cold, all business. Sam watched her in stupefied wonder. Moments ago he had sucked in deep breaths of relief to discover it hadn't been her employee ID, that she wasn't the one who burned Isaac and stonewalled Allison. But instead of getting Wendy back, it turns out he had lost two friends—pathetically, he thought, his *only* two friends. Nowhere in this plot he had been building in his head had it occurred to him both Wendy and Greg may not be on his side. Sam felt as if his legs were affixed to heavy weights. He barely had the energy to watch what was happening.

"I'm taking these, Charlie wants them secured right away," said Wendy, as she pulled the papers from Sam's hands.

Phil's tone was calm: "Look, I'm feeling really cut out of the communication loop." Sam was aware of Wendy extending her cell phone. "Want to call Charlie yourself?" Sam had never heard her sound more authoritative. He noticed Greg slinking away into the background, like he was trying to disappear.

The pitch of Phil's voice started to climb higher. "I need to get to this Republican Party National Security Forum thing. Charlie's speaking in a bit, and I have gladhandling to do. Did you drive here?" He was talking to Wendy like she was the help.

"Yes," Wendy replied.

"Okay, I need you and Daryl to take care of this. This is adversely affecting my energy." Phil moved his hands in the same circle motion as earlier. "You take them to that place we talked about until we can contact our people at the FBI."

Wendy shot Daryl an expectant smile and said, "Come with me." Sam thought about the watchtower, Daryl's eyes on Wendy, the way she'd taken his hand. Of course, Sam thought. They know each other, or they will know each other.

Daryl released his grip from Sam's shoulders and, for a moment, Sam was standing of his own volition, tall and weak, a fragile sapling. But then, a firm hand on the back of his neck. Daryl was pushing him through the door and onto the lawn, where grey light covered the brown stubble, and the air pricked his skin into goosebumps. Sam hadn't had time to look back at Greg, but he imagined him standing silently with his wife in an empty home.

Sam was walking, or being pushed, toward a small, black car two houses down. When Sam was twenty feet away he let out a vicious laugh. He and Allison thought they'd been so smart, that they'd outrun the black car. But there was Allison sitting in its back seat, head leaning back, hands zip-tied to the headrest of the seat in front of her. She was wearing the pained expression of someone trying to wake up from a bad dream.

"Daryl," said Wendy, "I imagine we should take my car, since you and Phil came together, and he's not, well, going to the same place as us?" She shot him a smile, a girlish giggle perceptible in her tone. The sparkle was back. "Besides, I'd rather not drive around in a mysterious black vehicle that looks like it belongs to an assassin."

Daryl awkwardly formed the shape of a pistol with his left hand and made a shooting motion at Wendy with his forefinger, somehow holding onto Sam with his left hand the whole time. So they're having so much fun, Sam thought to himself, as he felt Daryl's impossibly strong hands pushing him towards the bright blue Nissan parked behind the black car, then thrusting him into the back seat. Sam could feel the knife in his right pocket pressing into his thigh. He could reach for it, but not yet. Who knew what weapons Daryl was carrying.

Daryl went over to the black car to get Allison, his eyes on Wendy all the while. I could run for it, thought Sam, but he didn't dare, remembering the feeling of Daryl's thumb and forefinger digging into his shoulder, how that was all it had taken to hold him in place.

"Can you keep a close eye on them while I drive? Just tell me how to get there," Wendy said, catching Daryl's eye from the driver's seat. She paused, then smiled shyly. "Sorry, my car's a bit of a mess."

"Don't mind at all." Daryl was sitting in the passenger seat. And for the first time, Sam saw him smile.

In retrospect, Sam thought to himself, cynicism would have been the right play. I got baited into this by Allison, then Wendy calling me a phony. But a phony is what I am.

When Sam looked at Allison again, her face was grey. He thought back to the day he ran into his old comrade Francis on the streets of Chicago, barking at him about stopping a war. His fate, Sam thought, will be like mine: self-righteous busywork followed by disappointment, detention, or some combination of the two.

Chapter 20

In the back seat, still cuffed, Allison rubbed her foot against Sam's calf in a gesture of consolation. Her face was the softest he'd seen it—a look of pity, he realized, as he sat taller in his seat. They were driving fast, and Sam didn't bother to look where they were headed. An office, a jail cell, some farmhouse—the venue didn't matter. Either way, they were heading into FBI custody. Or maybe it was private security, or InfraGard—whatever that was. It didn't matter at this point.

Sam tried to block out the sound of Wendy and Daryl chattering in the front seat. Wendy's voice was intimate. She was doing most of the talking, Daryl responding in shy monosyllables.

"I'm starving. I could really use a bite to eat after this. Have you been to the Keg and Barrel since they switched management?"

"Can't say I have."

"It's the Bransens, the guys who also own LJ's Deli. Usually switching management is a disaster, but I heard they've actually fixed the place up. They're doing construction on the patio for the summer. I saw it when I drove by the other day. It looks really nice."

"Oh, they are?"

"Yeah, the old patio was falling apart." Wendy paused. "When we're done with this, I was going to go check it out. Been a long day."

"Sure has." Daryl stuttered. "Would you want some... company?" It seemed he could barely get the words out.

"Sure would." Wendy took her eyes off the road to give Daryl a long smile. Sam could see the profile of her high cheekbones and firm jaw where it gave way to the slope of her neck.

Sam looked over at Allison and rolled his eyes dramatically, looking to the left, then to the sky, then back around. Allison gave a half smile and shook her head, as if to say, we're both screwed, but you have it slightly worse than me. Sam felt something crack underneath his foot. A green crayon. He thought about Wendy's daughter scribbling out a vague approximation of a unicorn. Even then, he'd known deep down. But at least there had been a sliver of doubt.

Sam looked out of the window, not wanting Allison to see the tear moving in a straight line down his right cheek. These could have been the same cornfields he'd driven through with Keith and Wendy, or completely different. There were no other vehicles on the road. The only sound was the engine and wind resistance.

"Did you feel that?" Wendy sounded jittery.

"Feel what?" said Daryl.

"The car is shaking."

"It is?"

Sam looked at Allison, who gave a shrug. They were flying past an empty field, the sky starting to darken. Sam could see a small house, maybe a quarter mile up, its porch light on. He imagined a wheel flying off, the car spinning out of control. A moment ago, he hadn't felt he had much to lose, but now he pulled his seatbelt on, and quietly fastened Allison's too.

Dust flew past his window as the car slowed. Wendy was hitting the brakes as she directed the vehicle to the narrow shoulder. More skidding and dust, then the car stopped. Seconds later a truck flew past, the suction gently rattling the car frame.

Wendy put her head on the wheel then looked over at Daryl. "Of all possible timing, this is the worst. I think the air in one of the tires is low. I'm going to get out and check."

She moved to unbuckle her seatbelt, but Daryl reached over and put a hand on hers. "Let me do it."

"Really?" She looked over and smiled.

Sam almost snorted out loud. When had Wendy become such a princess? he wondered.

"I insist," said Daryl, and for the first time since he got in the car, he looked sure of himself.

"Thank you so much. There's a tire kit and a spare in the trunk if you need it."

"Let me look at the tires first."

Daryl stepped out, leaving the door open.

"This tire looks okay."

"Can you check the back one?"

"Sure."

Daryl was crouching right outside of Sam's window. Sam saw Wendy's eyes in the rearview, but she didn't seem to notice him. She was adjusting the mirror so she could see Daryl.

"I'm not seeing anything," Daryl shouted. "It looks like it might be a little low, but not enough—"

The window filled with dust. Sam heard a roar, then a slam. He thought they'd been hit, but then he saw brown fields zipping past the window. The passenger door was closed. Sam looked out of the back window. Daryl was slowly getting up and scratching his head, becoming smaller as the car sped away.

Both of Wendy's hands were on the wheel. She was upright and looking in the rearview. Watching Daryl.

When she flipped her head around to the back seat, her helpless smile was gone—something fierce in its place. "I'm guessing we have about ten minutes until Daryl finds a way to make a phone call."

"What's happening?" Sam couldn't catch his breath. The car was flying at what felt like ninety miles an hour.

"What do you think, you dork? She's helping us," Allison said.

"So, you're not... evil?" It came out higher pitched than Sam meant it to.

"No, I'm Anonymous64925. This was the only way I thought I could shake Rambo over there. He's had a thing for me for months so I figured I'd, I don't know, use it against him."

"So Charlie didn't send you?"

"You're a quick one, Sam."

Allison butted in. "How did you know where we were?"

"I was at the office helping Charlie prep for tonight's event. I overheard all his phone conversations with Phil. I figured you needed help beyond mysterious anonymous messages."

"God, well, thank you," said Allison. "They've been chasing us since we left the house on Sunnyside."

Wendy whipped her head around so quickly her hair was a few seconds behind. "You know about the house on—" she paused with indignation. "You were looking through my things?"

"It was on your bulletin board!" Sam squeaked. "I just happened to notice when we were posting Jessica's drawing, which I—"

Allison looked over at Sam, totally lost. "Who's Jessica?"

Wendy's stare pierced Sam through the rearview mirror. "I trusted you."

"I was investigating Charlie and, here, you have his name written down with a mysterious address in plain view, what was I—" Sam stopped himself. "For that matter, what were you doing with it?"

"I don't owe you an explanation, I rescued you. That's one of the perks of being the rescuer—you don't have to explain yourself to the rescuee."

Allison butted in. "Guys, guys. What difference does it

make? She's clearly on our side."

Wendy calmed down. "The address kept showing up on charity forms Charlie had me file, and Allison was poking me for suspicious things, so I jotted it down. I'd been looking at it every morning for a week before driving Jessica to school, asking my-self how far I wanted to go."

Sam wanted to apologize, or maybe just hold Wendy, but from the backseat all he could get out was an approximation of reassurance. "Look, Wendy—"

"When you have a five-year-old daughter it's not…"

"Yeah."

"But you guys kind of made the decision for me, so here I am. Let me guess, Sunnyside… it's an empty lot," said Wendy.

Allison took over for Sam. "Oh no, there's the general outline of a house, it just hasn't been lived in for forty years. But Charlie sure got a lot of money for it from the Healthy Futures Alliance."

Wendy let out an audible exhale.

As Sam looked out of the window, he felt his head spin. Or was this the vertigo coming back to visit him—the feeling that it doesn't matter whether you're still or moving, because nothing is the same.

When Sam turned back to Wendy, she was handing some-thing over the seat. It was pieces of paper, crumpled, but still intact. The internal memo, the field report.

Sam reached for them hesitantly, not sure whether Wendy was offering or angrily discarding them. Sam went to grab them, and as he did, he cupped Wendy's hand—just for a moment. The warmth of her fingers seemed to radiate up his arm. He didn't know it could feel so good to touch someone's hand. He slowly brushed his fingers down her hand until his fingertips were touching hers. He put the papers gently on his knees and wiped his cheek—still moist—with the back of his hand.

"I got to say, Wendy, wonderful performance." Allison said, nodding her head enthusiastically. "Even I was starting to hate you and I don't have a thinly veiled crush on you. I would clap if I weren't still tied to the back of your seat."

"I don't—" Sam started, sawing through the zipties with Greg's kitchen knife.

Wendy cut him off. "I have no idea where to go right now."

Allison held her newly uncuffed fingers a centimeter apart and mouthed to Sam: "Very thin."

"Any ideas would be great right now, I didn't plan past this part." Wendy sounded frantic. "Wait, I know. We'll go to Maggie's Diner."

"A restaurant?" Sam looked at Allison, who shrugged her shoulders, as if to say, I used up all of my options already. "Won't we be a bit, I dunno, exposed?"

"That's exactly the point. It's public, so if they try anything..." Wendy's voice trailed off. "Besides, I've never seen anyone from the Commission go there. It's too—"

Sam cut her off. "Lowbrow. I know. You told me last time."

Allison looked at Sam, then at Wendy in the front seat. "Ooh, some personal history I don't know about. Fascinating." Sam jabbed her with his elbow, and she dropped her grin. "I don't have a better idea. I'll tell my editor to meet us there."

Sam leaned toward Wendy. "Where's Jessica? Is she being watched by someone reliable?"

"Well, if you consider Mr. DUI reliable."

"Glad to hear it." Sam leaned back in his seat and took a long breath.

***

They were seated in a booth against the far wall, a few tables down from where Sam and Wendy had dined before. When the waiter came, Allison ordered a black coffee, and Sam asked for a horseshoe, smiling at Wendy, who was sitting across from him. When Wendy ordered a salad, Sam shot her a look of mock shock. "I can only eat that about once a year," she said. Sam figured neither of them could eat at all at a time like this, but he suspected that Wendy, like him, had worked in the restaurant business and knew taking up a table without ordering was rude.

As soon as the server left, Allison, sitting to Sam's right, said sharply, "Okay, we really need to figure this out. Publishing this story is the only protection we have and we're running out of time. If United's role in both causing and covering up the explosion comes to light, it won't matter what laws they say we broke."

"I want to see those documents," said Wendy. Sam laid them on the table, smoothing them gently. Wendy leaned her weight onto her elbows, her hair cascading over her eyes as she traced the words with a finger.

"So let me get this straight," said Allison. "United Gas uses the Healthy Futures Alliance to funnel money to Charlie by overpaying him for a house he bought on the cheap. In exchange, he blissfully ignores evidence that United Gas has major safety problems with God knows how many gas lines."

"But he doesn't just look the other way," Sam cut in.

"Right," Allison added. "He fires a staffer from inspections for raising the alarm. And he cuts off Little Miss Anonymous over here from accessing the safety reports, right around the time he gets a payment of $1.2 million for some shitty building he couldn't sell for the cost of a new SUV."

Allison nodded at Wendy, who brushed the hair out of her eyes and said, "And then when a gas line explodes, and someone actually dies, the company and Commission use the hysterical climate to insinuate—without evidence—that the blast could have been caused by terrorists. And they've got a direct line to an FBI office—InfraGard—and Eagle Security. In the name of fighting terrorism, public law enforcement and private mercenaries hunt down whistleblowers. Meanwhile, it's United Gas—not terrorists—that poses a safety threat. Their gas lines are ticking time bombs in thousands of buildings across the state."

"We have the evidence," Allison quipped back. "We just have to tell the story."

"You're not the only writer here," said Sam. "I still have testimony to file."

"Sam, you know you'll never get a chance to do that," Wendy said. "This story will have to be your testimony."

Wendy picked up the papers from the table and put them in her lap to clear the way for a busser to put down glasses of ice water. He had close-cut hair and calloused hands. He gave a polite nod to Sam before turning away. Sam looked at Wendy.

"Didn't we see that guy last time? He seems familiar."

"Oh, I don't know."

"He seemed like he recognized me."

"Sure, maybe."

"Sam, I need you to focus." Allison snapped her fingers in front of him, like she was trying to get the attention of a puppy.

"Okay, yeah, I'm sorry. It seems pretty cut-and-dry. What more do we need?"

"I'm not so sure," said Wendy. "It's hard to believe that the IRS or some other body wouldn't have caught wind of this. Aren't groups like the Healthy Futures Alliance audited? You can't just hand over money from a not-for-profit organization to bribe someone. How would you write that down in your annual report?"

"Yeah, it still feels like there's something we're missing," said Allison. She caught sight of someone through the window and waved invitingly at the door. A short woman with salt and pepper hair that reached in tight ringlets down to her chin approached the table.

Sam stood to greet her, extending his hand. "You must be Allison's esteemed editor."

"Judith." Her hand squeezed his with a firm grip.

Judith sat next to Wendy, and Allison explained everything. When she stopped, Judith was shaking her head, her curls bouncing like popcorn on a stove. "I just don't think you have it yet. You need to know the mechanism for disbursing bribe money. The Healthy Futures Alliance is highly respected and vouched for. I attended one of their fundraisers. The chief of police was there, city counselors. We can't just insinuate they're a front organization if we don't even understand how."

Allison restrained her voice. "We have proof the payment was sent at the same time Wendy lost access to those reports. How much longer do you want us to wait? For another person to die? You know how many people are impacted by their faulty gas lines?" Allison pointed at a "Springfield Together" sign on the back wall. It was on a posterboard written in careful penmanship, below it a small drawing of an American flag.

Judith looked up at Allison and put out an arm, her baggy charcoal-grey sweater spreading like a wing. "I'm sorry. What you have is wonderful, a potential bombshell, but you're not there yet. You need to make sure you have the story. You should try reaching out to the Healthy Futures Alliance. Go through their 990 forms. Maybe you can find some inside sources. There might even be the possibility of a FOIA."

"But we need to do this now. They're looking for us. We have to go public before they—" Allison stopped herself.

"I'm sorry, Allison. We can't rush this. But I'll reach out to our lawyer now to see if she has any thoughts."

Allison looked down at her hands, which were clasped in front of her, elbows on the table, her right foot bouncing. Sam and Wendy were both watching her.

"I'm sorry," said Judith. "I have to go."

Wendy and Sam watched as Judith shut the door behind her with a jingle. Allison had her forehead in her hands. "She's right," said Allison, her voice betraying her exhaustion. "We're not quite there yet. We have no inside sources, no real knowledge of how money moves around in the organization. And we have no time."

"What do we do?" asked Wendy. "You said the story is our best protection."

The busser put a plate in front of Sam. He inhaled a cloud of greasy steam, but his appetite was gone.

Sam looked at the busser as he walked away. He had a tired gait, rocking from side to side as he moved on to the next table. I wonder how long his shift has been today, Sam thought, as he rubbed the burn on his forefinger with his thumb. I don't miss those days working in a restaurant. Too bad that a scholarship recipient is stuck here waiting tables, when he should be off reading Voltaire and James Baldwin and writing essays about alienated labor.

"Wait, that's it," Sam gasped. In one swift motion, Sam pulled his backpack onto his lap and opened the zipper. His hand fumbled for the crumpled up Healthy Futures scholarship brochure he knew he'd find in one of its crevices, among caked-in crumbs and balled-up receipts. He pulled out a folded piece of paper and hastily opened it up, but it was the anti-war rally flyer Francis had handed him all those months ago on that hot summer day, before it all got messy. Its creases were so worn they left faded lines running through the heavy black ink. He wasn't sure why, but he'd look at it from time to time—his own personal talisman, or maybe just a reminder. Shoving it back in the backpack, he found the Healthy Futures Alliance brochure and slammed it on the table.

"What are you doing?" The spark was gone from Allison's voice.

"The scholarships that Mrs. Belinda was complaining about. That's how they did it."

As Sam read from the brochure, Allison's eyes widened. "Of course." She bolted up from the booth and ran towards the door. Sam sprinted close behind her.

The sky was the color of iron ore. A parked car was turning on its lights. Allison ran to it and banged on the window.

"Judith, we have the mechanism. They're not paying out the scholarships. They set impossible standards for getting the money. Now it all makes sense."

When Sam got to the window, Judith was staring at Allison, her eyes narrowed into half-moons.

"How do you mean?"

Sam held out the brochure, and read from it rapidly. "30-hour work weeks, GPA of 3.9, extracurriculars. They make it impossible for any of these kids to hit these markers, so they can award them the scholarships to move money but never actually pay it out. It's on their books as an expense for the fiscal year because it's a nominal cost but then the next year, when they file taxes, it's back on the other side of the ledger."

"So, you have sources saying so?"

"Six," Sam butted in. "I think. If we can get Mrs. Belinda to help us."

"Mrs. who?" said Judith.

"A source," said Allison.

"You think you could get comment from those six people tonight?"

"We're sure as shit gonna try," Allison replied. "I've lived and breathed and eaten this story for over a year. I'm positive I could type it out in forty-five minutes, tops, once I get my sources. It could go live before midnight."

Judith shook her head. "That's not the only issue. We can't publish until we reach out to United Gas and the Commission for comment. We have to give them a chance to respond to every single allegation laid out in detail."

"Oh, right, I'm going to call up the mercenaries who just tried to disappear me to some black site and ask for their side of the story? Why don't I invite them to trace my call while I'm at it?"

"Allison, this isn't funny. These are the most powerful people in the state. We can't just go after them without due diligence. People like United are litigious. Just one libel lawsuit could—"

Allison cut her off. "They can't win a libel lawsuit, because nothing will be untrue. Every single word I write will be accurate."

"They don't have to win it. The lawsuit itself, and a few calls to our board, are enough to jeopardize your job—and mine." Judith bowed her head, and when she looked up, her expression was sheepish. "I'm sorry. I can't budge on this. We need to run all of this by our lawyer."

"But—"

"It's not just your job on the line."

Allison took a step backwards. Her cheeks were red, eyes angry embers. "Fine. If it's a comment you want, Sam, let's go get a comment."

Chapter 21

Sam peered at Wendy from the passenger seat as she drove. When she looked at him, he turned his gaze to the yellow road markings flying at the car. He strained to hear Allison on the phone in the back seat.

"You're right. We should have come to you sooner," Allison was saying.

"We need their names and contact information. But more importantly, could you call them? See if they'd talk? The turn-around is so tight. And we'd like to use you as a source. Mrs. Belinda—"

The tires roared against the road. Sam pressed his thumb to the burn on his forefinger.

"There's nothing we know that we haven't told you." Allison paused. "Yeah, I've got them right here. We're all going together."

Allison exhaled. "Thank you so much. I'll call as soon as it's over."

The car turned into the Springfield High School parking lot. Wendy parked the car at the far side of the lot. In the silent car, they shared a moment of hesitation, all three staring at the front doors.

Sam looked over at Wendy. Her spine was straight, chin angled upwards. "You sure you want to go through with this?"

"It's either pulling this off or five to fifteen years in federal prison, so I think we're past 'want' at this point."

"Right."

"Is it really courage when you have no choice?" Wendy let out a slight laugh and opened her door to exit. "Come on, let's nail these pricks."

**

When Sam pushed open the front doors, he found Angelo standing in front of a trophy case with three men and one woman. They were all wearing suits. Angelo's jacket was the color of fog, a black button-up shirt beneath it.

"What are you doing here?" asked Sam. Standing closer, he could see one of the glass panels of the trophy case was missing. Hastily taped-on cardboard masked the damage caused by the exploded gas pipe.

"They're going to commemorate Raphael after the Q&A. The union is turning out," said Angelo. "What are you doing here? Word is, security is looking for you."

"You heard?" said Sam.

"We hear everything," Angelo said. "You here for the forum,

too?"

"You could say that. Which way is the auditorium?"

"There's a lot of security there, Sam. You sure you want to go?"

"Yeah, we're sure," said Allison, standing just behind Sam. Wendy was silent. Sam gave a single nod.

"Well then, why don't we take you around back. Maya, do you mind showing him?"

Angelo turned to the woman, who was short and slim, with dyed red hair tumbling out of a high ponytail. She gave Sam and his motley crew a once over and raised a single eyebrow at Angelo.

"You can trust him," Angelo assured Maya. "He's the only person from the Commission who showed up to Raphael's funeral."

Maya sized them up one last time then, in a Spanish accent, commanded, "Okay, follow me."

She started walking rapidly down the hallway, and Sam, Wendy, and Allison followed behind. They walked through a metal door and into a narrow room lined with lockers against both walls, a long wooden bench between them. As they walked past, Sam saw that each locker had a small placard engraved with a name. Al, Sylvia, Martin...

Raphael. Sam stopped.

He turned around at the pressure of a hand on his shoulder. Wendy was staring at Raphael's name on the locker door.

"Come on, let's go," said Maya, holding a door open on the other side of the room.

The door let them out into the back left of a massive room. Maya didn't follow. The seats sloped downward towards the stage, separated into sections by three aisles, a microphone at each. The front of the room was full, the back half peppered with people, the walls a sickly shade of beige.

"You take that aisle," Allison whispered to Sam, pointing to the pathway that ran down the middle of the room. "Wendy, you go there. Allison pointed at the aisle on the far right. "I want one of us in each line for the mic. I'm not positive, but I think they're doing questions and answers now."

As Sam walked towards the microphone at the center of the room, he could hear the crunching of the documents folded in his pocket. To his left were three news cameras, intern types—all of them young men—huddled behind them. Sam shook his head. He hadn't believed Allison that local news stations would be lining up to air this event live, but he'd forgotten this was Springfield.

About twenty feet in front of him was a stage with a table. Behind it, flat against the wall, the sort of large American flag you would see draped over a football field on a Friday night. Dangling from the table was a banner that read, "Central Illinois Republicans National Security Forum sponsored by Zenith Defense." Charlie was sitting at the far right of the table, leaning into a microphone. On the far left was the police chief from the news conference. In the middle, a man with rounded, combed-back hair, rivers of gray running through it. Sam squinted at the placard in front of him: U.S. Rep. Adam Wagner.

"He's the civil servant, not me," Charlie was saying, his voice booming to the high ceiling as he pointed at Adam Wagner. "I don't think there's anything extraordinary about trying to give back to the next generation. It's something all of us do, all the time, most of us in obscurity." When he stopped talking, he had a satisfied smile on his face.

"Representative, how would you answer that question?" said the police chief, his jaw perpetually angling upward. "What kind of leadership do you think the Republican Party needs today?"

Adam Wagner put his elbows on the table and leaned forward. "When you ask about the kind of leadership we need today, a few words come to mind. National unity. Security." Wagner waited for the applause to stop. "That's my mandate as I represent the voters from the land of Abraham Lincoln, who was no stranger to trying times."

Sam's eyes wandered around the room. He saw Wendy at the microphone in the next aisle. She was pitched forward like a frightened schoolchild. About ten rows in front of her, Phil sat with his right ankle on his left knee, phone open in his hand. He seemed entirely unfazed by the day's events. Thomas French sat next to him—they were the richest-looking people in the room. Most of the crowd seemed more haggard, like Ashley's parents, their faces leathered and cracked by work.

"Just days ago, we suffered our own devastating explosion right here in this city, in the very place our young people are supposed to feel most safe and protected—this school." Wagner seemed to be speaking more to the cameras than the room. "And it's a testament to the courage and tenacity of this city that we are gathered here today, at the site of the explosion, with an investigation ongoing, to talk about making our communities safer. We need the kind of leadership that can hold our communities together, keep the fabric of society whole, and show those who would harm us that we won't back down."

The room erupted into applause. Charlie, slowly clapping his hands, was looking at Sam, or just behind him, Sam couldn't tell.

His face didn't register any recognition—the stage lights were too bright for them to notice their faces, Sam assumed.

"Well, I thought that was the last question, but it looks like we have a few more people in line," said the police chief, facing the crowd.

Sam looked over at Allison. There was one woman in front of her.

The young man called on the line to Sam's left, and the woman in front of Allison stepped forward. "Mr. Representative, is it true you're planning to recruit a candidate to replace Burns in two years?"

Good, Sam thought, Allison will be called next. It'll be her, not me. Still, while the woman asked her question, he silently practiced what they'd all agreed to say.

The Representative was talking, but Sam was having difficulty paying attention. He bounced on his feet, worried that if he stopped he'd fall forward. "Look, it's no secret I've been disenchanted with Senator Burns for some time," said Adam Wagner. "The airport maneuver was really the straw that broke the camel's back."

When the Representative was done, Sam was enveloped in applause. The room seemed to be crowding in on him. His legs felt rubbery. He looked down at his feet and took deep breaths.

When he looked up, it was silent. Everyone was staring at him.

"Did you have a question, young man?" asked the police chief.

Sam looked over at Allison. She was shoving her hands towards him, the motion of someone trying to hand off a baton.

"My name is Sam Golden, and I'm an analyst with the Illinois Commerce Commission." Sam spoke slowly into the microphone, which boomed and crackled, whistling with every consonant. "I've got my question right here." Sam reached into his pocket. He saw Charlie try to catch the attention of the police chief with a flick of his right hand, but the chief didn't see. His jaw was angled at Sam, waiting.

"I have a question for Charlie Harper, of the Illinois Commerce Commission." Sam saw Thomas French and Phil's heads whip in his direction. "Did you knowingly conceal this evidence that United's gas lines are decrepit, falling apart, and liable to explode, in exchange for receiving $1.2 million from United Gas, funneled through the Healthy Futures Alliance?" Sam held the internal memo and field safety report towards the stage. The paper was shaking enough for the rattling sound to echo through the PA system.

"And is it true that you fired Isaac Jones from the Illinois Commerce Commission's inspections department for trying to expose the public safety threat?" Sam's voice came out louder this time. It sounded smooth and strong. He liked the way it filled the room.

Sam saw Phil stand up and then sit back down. The police chief was looking at Charlie, who drew his forefinger to one side of his neck and pulled it across to the opposite side.

"Alright, it looks like we have a disruptor in the crowd." The police chief sounded like someone who'd told many people to sit down and shut up. "We're going to move to the next microphone."

The chief pointed at Allison's line. She was standing in front. "I'm a reporter for the Springfield Weekly, here to get comment

245

for a story set to go live before midnight. Firstly, I'd like you to answer the questions presented by my colleague, Sam Golden. Secondly, I'd like to see if you have any response to the allegation that United Gas knowingly used the Healthy Futures Alliance to funnel funds for the purpose of bribing you, Charlie Harper, to turn a blind eye to widespread public safety concerns. And I'd like to know your response to the allegation that you skimmed off payouts to scholarship recipients in order to cover your trail. I am happy to share with you a list of six scholarship recipients who were never paid the amounts they were promised."

Allison turned toward Phil and Thomas French, who were both looking at her, and pointed her finger, like a prosecutor in a courtroom. "I would like to address all of the above questions to Thomas French and Phil of United Gas. Consider this your request for comment before our piece is posted online later tonight."

Thomas French and Phil turned away and looked at the stage. Sam couldn't see a single muscle in their bodies move.

"I, uh, I'm... What the hell is going on here?" Charlie mumbled. Sam saw security guards walking towards Allison, but when they got close, they hovered, seemingly afraid to grab her. One of them pulled the plug on her microphone.

Sam turned around, towards the news cameras, and held the papers out so that they filled the lenses of two of the three cameras. One of the young men said weakly, "You're in my way." But no one did anything to stop him.

Charlie leaned in with a laugh, "Sounds like we have a conspiracy theory convention going on. I want to apologize to all you good people here, these things are hard to manage at public forums."

A voice rang out through the room. It started small but then grew larger. It was coming from the far-right aisle. "My name is Wendy, and I am Charlie Harper's assistant at the Illinois Commerce Commission. What is your response to the allegation that, when you received $1.2 million from United Gas, you cut off my access to inspection reports for United Gas? And is it true that our personal liberty is at risk just because we're exposing this, right here, right now? What is your response to the allegation that you sent a private security firm and public law enforcement after us under the guise of fighting terrorism?" Those last words came out harsh and shrill. Sam could feel them vibrate down his spine.

Sam thought Wendy was done, but when she started again there were daggers in her voice. "I worked for you for six years. I got your coffee, I picked your son up from practice, I renewed your country club membership. Whatever illusion I had that I could change things from the inside, or by taking small steps, is gone now. Because your greatest weapon is your absence. It is being on the golf course. It is having me pick up your laundry. All you have to do is nothing, and you're the company's best friend. I looked at the address on my bulletin board every morning for a week and kept—"

"Ok." A still smug Charlie leaned into the mic, "This woman is clearly losing it. Can we please get—"

"Shut up. I'm not done." She collected herself. "To think it has come to this—an explosion that killed someone, in the place children are supposed to feel most safe. I have a daughter. It could have been her school, it could have been her. For God's sake, you have a son."

It took everything Sam had to keep holding the documents to the news cameras. He wanted to run to her. To think I suspected her of being on the wrong side, he thought. And here she is, Elizabeth Gurley Flynn in business casual.

247

Sam felt a hand on his shoulder. It was firm and wiry. It had him pinned.

Before Sam could turn around, someone was pulling his hands together behind his back. Cuffs were being placed around his wrists—he couldn't tell if they were metal or plastic zip-ties. He looked over his shoulder at Wendy. A security guard was cuffing her. Sam couldn't see her face, but he imagined it crumpling. It's hard not to cry when you're being arrested, even if it's for a planned civil disobedience. There's something terrifying about the total lack of control over your own person.

But when the guard swung Wendy around, Sam was surprised by the defiant expression on her face. Her shoulders somehow seemed broader. Even in handcuffs, a guard gripping her arm, she wasn't crumpling—she was expanding. He smiled widely, even as he could feel his hands swell in the tight cuffs.

Sam looked to his left. Allison was being cuffed. She looked calm.

They were pushing Sam away from the stage, towards the large, oak door in the back. He still hadn't seen the person behind him, but he imagined he looked like the others—wearing a white uniform and navy blue hat, the mall cop version of Eagle Security. "Sir, we're taking you into custody." Sam heard a low voice in his ear.

"Where are you taking me?"

"Sangamon County Jail."

"You're not a police officer."

"I have the authority to make arrests. The police are on their way."

Sam heard a voice boom from the stage. "I categorically and unequivocally deny every one of these crazy allegations."

Sam turned his body around, getting enough momentum to shake off the security guard. He looked at Charlie and shouted so the room could hear him. "We have all the evidence. It's already been broadcast on two local media stations. Isaac Jones' Field Safety Report, in which he testifies that United Gas' gas lines are falling apart system-wide. We also have the memo he wrote to you in warning about the public danger."

The guards rushing towards Sam paused as Charlie leaned into the mic to speak. "I don't care what you think you have. There is something called the rule of law, and if you had any leg to stand on, you wouldn't have had to break it. But this is something you already know a thing or two about. I know about your past, Sam. Your arrests, your New York sensibilities. You hate this town and everyone in it, it's obvious to everyone who's met you."

"You're right, Charlie." Sam looked down and took a long breath. "At least you were right. I did hate this town—at first. But it turns out I just hate the people running it. Everyone else is actually pretty great—with a thousand stories of courage and humor and kindness and defiance."

"Touching." Charlie turned to the police chief. "Get 'em the hell out of here!"

Sam was once more being shoved back towards the door. For a moment, he lost his balance, and he thought he'd fall onto the empty seat next to him. But he kept walking—or being pushed—forward.

Sam saw the guard reach his right hand over to push the door, his left hand holding Sam by the cuffs. Nothing happened.

The guard pushed again. It didn't move.

The guard let go of Sam, backed up, then rammed shoulder first into the door. He fell back from the impact, stumbling to catch himself.

Free of his grip, Sam turned around. He heard a woman's voice, but he wasn't sure where it was coming from.

"No one's going anywhere until you hear from us. Our SEIU union brothers and sisters have chained the door."

Sam looked at Wendy. She was also whipping her head around trying to determine where the sound was coming from. Allison stared toward the front of the room.

About six men and one woman stood on stage to the left of the panelists. Sam squinted. He recognized Angelo's fog-colored suit and black and silver hair. He stood in the middle of the pack, his arms crossed in front of him. Maya was speaking into a microphone she had commandeered from the police chief, her voice climbing in pitch.

"My name is Maya de Lugo. Our union brother Raphael Sanchez is dead, and you're not going anywhere until you answer their questions."

Charlie seemed smaller, collapsing in on himself. In a thin voice, he said, "You can't keep us here. It's a fire hazard."

"What?" Maya shouted. "Is there something wrong with the pipes?"

"Get them out of here. All of them." Charlie was shouting into the microphone, waving his hands towards the sanitation workers. The guards started moving slowly in their direction, but they seemed unsure of themselves.

"The whole city of Springfield is watching." Her hands cuffed, Allison nodded towards the news cameras. The faintest smile spread across her face.

Sam noticed a security guard pull a toolbox from beneath the stage. He reached for bolt cutters. Their time was limited.

Allison continued, "My—our—story, with plenty of evidence and testimony, is going online tonight. You can't stop it, even if you throw us in jail. My editor's watching right now on live TV, and she has all the information we do. What's it gonna be?"

"You want my comment?" Charlie snapped.

A soft murmur rippled through the crowd.

"My comment is…"

Sam felt himself grinding his teeth.

"No comment. There'll be no teary-eyed confessions tonight. Everything you've alleged today is a total fiction, and your little janitor friends here locking the doors isn't going to change that. Now publish whatever you want." Charlie crossed his arms in front of him as the police chief and Adam Wagner watched, confusion spreading across their faces.

Sam saw Thomas French and Phil whispering to each other in their own private conference.

Then Charlie's hands dropped to his side. Someone was moving in front of the stage, gesturing with his arms. He had an expensive suit and groomed, wavy hair. Phil. He was standing now, Thomas French still sitting in his seat.

"If the Commerce Commission has evidence that our gas

lines are in anything less than perfect condition, we would like to know," Phil shouted, so that his voice carried across the room.

What is he up to? wondered Sam.

"We do our best, but we have a giant network, and we can't know everything at once. If we're going to begin to heal the hurt in this town, we must fully cooperate with the investigation and share everything—I mean everything—we know. Terrorism hasn't been ruled out, but neither has a compromised gas line." Phil had been slowly turning his body so that he now looked straight into the camera, eyes locked with thousands of imaginary Springfieldians. His hand was on his heart, his eyes sparkling with what could be tears.

Thomas French had reclined so far into his seat Sam could only see his blonde comb-over, which didn't move. Charlie's voice was no longer mic'ed, and the words he formed were not loud enough to hear. But Sam thought he saw him mouth, "Phil, you slimy son of a bitch."

The murmur in the room rose again. Sam saw heads turn left, then right. In the sea of color and motion, Phil was still.

Allison attempted to fight off the security guard detaining her. Sam could hear her voice rising above the murmur. "Don't listen to a word this man says."

"Have we met?" said Phil. "The Springfield Weekly, right? I'm a huge fan of alternative media. You asked for my comment. United Gas pledges to cooperate with any and all investigations into the state of our pipes. As far as the allegations about the Healthy Futures Alliance, if any of the money we generously donated was misallocated, we join the public in demanding to know. We're happy to support you and any other media outlets in calling for all these allegations to be followed up."

"Have we met? You had me detained an hour ago," Allison shouted from across the room. "United has been orchestrating the whole thing." She turned to the cameras, "Don't let him spin this."

The press didn't budge. Everyone remained focused on Phil as Allison was escorted toward the exit near her, hands pulled tightly behind her back. Sam looked over his shoulder. He could see Wendy being pushed through a door by a security guard following close behind.

Sam saw Phil approach the stairs to the right of the stage. He walked past Wagner and Charlie, who was shouting wordlessly in the din, but Phil didn't seem to notice. When he reached the police chief, Phil bent down and whispered something in his ear.

The chief stood up and, for a moment, seemed unsure of what to do next. But then he walked in Charlie's direction, arms swinging deliberately, as if to steady himself.

Sam saw the chief place a hand on Charlie's shoulder. Charlie grew quiet, stood up, and the two walked together off the stage, towards the exit Wendy had just been pushed through. The chief led Charlie, his head bowed, through the doorway.

Phil walked over to Maya and put a hand on her lower back before taking the microphone from her hands. He stood like an actor on a stage at three quarters position, addressing Maya, but also the crowd. "First of all, I want to thank you for being here. I was already planning to take this occasion to announce that United will make a generous donation to the remembrance fund of your Local in Raphael's honor." Phil gave Maya a wide grin, but she returned it with a skeptical expression. The other janitors were standing behind her, arms crossed, like a security detail.

Phil turned so that he directly faced the microphone. "These allegations are serious and frankly, if true, United would be the party most harmed, since it's allegedly our money that's been stolen, money we intended for at-risk youth," he said.

Of course, Sam thought to himself. Phil was turning on Charlie, Greg, and everyone at the Commission who had helped launder United's negligence. Phil, being the world-class spinster he was, saw which way the wind was blowing and decided it best to get out ahead of this.

A closed-mouth laugh caught in Sam's throat as he felt pain jolt up his right elbow. The room was in motion, that familiar sinking and floating feeling, vertigo back to visit him. But this time there was someone else. The guard dug his fingers into both of Sam's forearms as he shoved him through the door.

Chapter 22

Sam walked up to window seven at the Sangamon County Jail. Greg was on the other side, sitting in a chair, his body disappearing into his orange jumpsuit. Greg's cheekbones formed hard angles, and his eyes looked larger in a smaller face, giving him the appearance of a frightened fawn. He had lost quite a bit of weight in just three months.

When Sam sat down, they both reached for their phones. His mouth was on the receiver, but Sam said nothing.

"I got the book you sent me. I liked it," said Greg.

"Oh, good."

"*For Whom the Bell Tolls*. A man questioning his faith while on a suicide mission only to push through. Read it when I was sixteen for school but didn't appreciate it until…"

"Yeah."

"Jail's much harder than I thought it would be."

Sam looked at the wall behind Greg. It was the beige of worn school bus seats. "How's Ashley?"

"About to burst. She's still on bedrest, so it's been hard for her to come. Her parents have made it a lot though." Greg looked down at his lap, then back up at Sam. "The call could come any day."

"Jesus, Greg." Sam paused. "How long are you going to be in here?"

"Until I go to trial or they force a plea deal out of me. A guy I know has been here a year and a half waiting for trial. I don't have $10,000 sitting around to make bail, and I'm not taking that from my in-laws—not now. I'm not like Charlie. He made bail right away, right?"

"He was back playing golf at the Aberdeen country club in no time."

"Can't believe he and I are the only people who got pinned for bribery. Oh and Keith, that poor sucker from inspections. Looks like they're trying to scapegoat him for the missing safety reports."

"Yeah," said Sam. "Worst part is that Keith was a true believer. He thought he was on the front lines of fighting terrorism from the perch of the Illinois Commerce Commission. 'Captain America' is what Wendy and I called him. Did everything by the book and nothing more than what he was asked to do. Angelo got cut loose, too."

"The janitor?"

"He's not facing charges, but he lost his job after the whole chaining-the-doors incident. An act of negligence, they fired him with cause. The union's taking up a collection."

"No one's jumping to take a collection for me," Greg said with a sharp laugh. Sam said nothing. "How did United get away with this?" asked Greg, sadly.

"Looking at all the evidence, there was nothing directly tying them to the Commission's wrongdoing. In our frantic rush to get the story out and expose them we never paused to notice how well United covered its tracks, how they kept themselves distant."

"But they were orchestrating the whole thing, those pricks—"

"All verbal, nothing on paper. I know they were, obviously you know. But a grand jury has no way of knowing beyond our testimony and a real estate deal gone bad. In any event, the stooge they replaced Charlie with asked me to come back. They were willing to ignore the 'stolen documents' for the P.R. value of having me on their side. Apparently my face on the internal investigation would lend it credibility with legislators and good government types."

"You're kidding."

Sam let out a chuckle. "Came with a hefty raise too. A raise so big it could in, say, a third world country be misconstrued as—"

"Hush money?"

"I was going to say a bribe, but yeah. I took the job for a whole thirty-six hours and just couldn't be a part of that. My mother thinks I'm crazy. You, the fall guy, and everyone else saves face. Allison—"

Greg cut him off. "The reporter?"

"Her story was pretty big. Of course, the editors wouldn't let her publish beyond the scope of the documents themselves, so Phil was left out of it and even spun himself as a champion of the investigation. But she, well, she doesn't drop things. She thinks she'll find something. Says she's working with some independent media center in Champaign-Urbana on some big exposé. We'll see."

Greg put the phone down below the separation glass, took a deep breath, then raised it back up to his ear. "Was it all for nothing?"

"No. Maybe some of those pipes will get fixed. Maybe one less person will die in some explosion. Or if someone does die, it'll be harder for them to call it terrorism. Maybe some of those kids will finally get their scholarship money. One Springfield is happy to have this out in the open. Mrs. Belinda said—"

"But the system is the same," Greg cut in. "The figureheads of United are the same. Or as you would put it, the 'capitalist class.'"

"Well, all we can do is try to change that. People are all we've got, whether we like it or not. We have to try."

"Try?" said Greg. "Trying is important. I like that." Greg paused, fingers working a fraying hem of his jumpsuit. "I bet a part of you is glad to see me in here though, no? I burned you bad. At least that's some justice."

"What does this help? You're just a grunt who can't make bail."

"Well, don't flatter me."

Sam let out a chuckle. "I'll send you another book soon, okay?"

"Thanks." Greg hung up the phone, and Sam did the same.

Sam stood up and walked to his left. He punched his code into a small locker and pulled out his possessions one by one, first his wallet, then his cell phone. He reached his hand in again and felt along the back-right corner.

When he pulled out the key, he stood for a moment, studying its circular keychain resting upright in his palm. "Home of Lincoln" in block letters, over a silhouette of the man himself. Sam let out a faint smile as he tossed the keychain a foot in the air and caught it palm-down, as if performing a trick for a child, before slipping it into his back pocket.

Sam walked over to a glass barrier and held his ID up. A corrections officer studied it then pressed a button, and a door opened to Sam's left.

On the other side was a sidewalk covered in slush the color of cigarette ash. Sam passed through a gate covered in barbed wire, then turned left at the road until he reached a bright blue Nissan.

Sam opened the door and sat down in the passenger seat.

"Hey, how'd it go?" Wendy's left forearm was on the steering wheel, her right hand reaching for Sam's knee.

Sam grabbed her fingers. They were small and warm.

"It was, well..."

"Depressing?"

"Yeah."

A tiny hand reached behind Sam's seat and tapped him on the shoulder. "That took so long," said Jessica. "Mommy had to

259

drive around the block in circles."

"It's true. The police wouldn't let me sit here," said Wendy.

Sam turned around until he was facing the back seat. "I appreciate that you waited so patiently. And you know what that means?"

"Ice cream?" Jessica was smiling so big Sam could see her molars.

"You bet. We'll stop in Pontiac. It's about halfway to Chicago. If you're extra good, you can get hot fudge."

"On the way back, too?"

"Well don't get ahead of yourself," Wendy said, shooting Sam a grin.

Sam reached into his coat pocket and uncrumpled the flyer that Francis had given him last summer when he'd run into him in the street. "No war!" it said in big black letters at the top. "Chicago February 15 peace march. Ten million people expected worldwide."

He put it on the cup holder between him and Wendy.

She turned the ignition and the car sputtered on. Sam moved his hand to her knee and gave her a squeeze. She pressed the gas.

About the Authors

Peter Lazare (1952-2018) was an expert analyst at the Illinois Commerce Commission in Springfield, Illinois for twenty years, and was simultaneously the co-owner of Grab-a-Java coffee shop with his wife, Meg Evans Lazare. He was known throughout the greater Springfield community for the artful and witty banners he displayed outside of the two Grab-a-Java locations, which often offered searing commentary. An original thinker with a keen intellect and an always-illuminating sense of humor, Peter was constantly engaged in study and endlessly curious about the world around him. He lived many lives: During his earlier years, Peter protested the Vietnam War, organized for the labor movement, and worked as a socialist organizer in a Chicago garment factory in the late '70s and early '80s. He was a dedicated father, brother, husband, grandfather, son, and friend who took seriously the charge to protect the human chain.

Sarah Lazare is a journalist. She lives in Chicago where she works as a reporter and web editor for the labor magazine, In These Times.

Acknowledgments

Thank you to Meg Evans Lazare, my mom, for believing in this project from the get-go, for loving it as much as I do, for eagerly reading each chapter as it came in, and for your endless dedication to ensuring dad's work lives on. Dad loved you to the moon and so do I.

Thank you to Jack Phelps, Sophia Lazare, Brook Celeste, Audrey Todd, Kate Walsh, and Chip Gibbons for being such trustworthy and thoughtful readers, and thanks so much to Nicky Guerreiro for your incredible editing talents. Ryan Grim, I really appreciate your enthusiasm and support for this project from the moment I reached out to you. Thank you to Bill Johnson, a dear friend of my dad's, for patiently helping me understand the inscrutable world of Illinois utilities regulation.

Thank you to Adam Johnson, my love, for holding me tight during the most devastating period of my life, for making sure I never had to grieve my dad alone, for somehow always finding a way to make me laugh. The endless hours you spent helping me map out complex plot lines, telling me what worked and what didn't, punching up dialogue, and poring through multiple revisions were the greatest possible gift you could have given me and my dad. When I was in the tall grass, you reached for my hand. And you haven't let go since.

Most of all, thank you to my dad, who blazed the path forward, always willing to take risks and try new things, including this book. I miss my dad every day and will cling tightly to his memory for the rest of my life. I am convinced he had many books in him, and I am so glad this one will see the light of day.

Testimony